STRONG VINCENT

— PRAISE FOR —
STRONG VINCENT

"Strong Vincent's actions on Little Round Top on July 2, 1863, have become the stuff of legend: his decision on his own authority to dispatch his brigade, his 'You can't retreat' injunction to Col. Joshua Chamberlain as he sent him to occupy the left flank, and his subsequent mortal wounding while directing his troops. Much less well-known are the events that built his character and the military experiences that led to Little Round Top. Author John Hinman truly brings Vincent to life. Like all good historical fiction writers, Hinman sticks close to the documented narrative but uses a fiction writer's craft to flesh out the story. Hinman, a retired English teacher, knows his Civil War history but he is also an excellent storyteller. This book is a terrific introduction to one of the Civil War's great heroes."

—LEON REED, author of *Stories the Monuments Tell: A Photo Tour of Gettysburg, Told by its Monuments*, and *History in Granite and Bronze: The Civil War Artwork of Gettysburg, Antietam, and Washington, DC*

"Hinman does an excellent job mixing local history in with Strong Vincent's story and doesn't rush through his life. The reader also gets a good sense of how Strong Vincent, already a leader and mature for his age, developed as a tactician. Thoroughly enjoyable."

—JEFF BLOODWORTH, professor of American Political History, Gannon University

"A fun read, well-paced read! The use of dialogue educates the reader. Bravo to John Hinman!"

—DR. JOE BEILEIN, associate professor of history, Penn State Behrend College

Strong Vincent: A Call to Glory

by John Hinman

© Copyright 2024 John Hinman

ISBN 979-8-88824-379-4

All rights reserved. No part of this publication may be reproduced, stored in a retrieval system, or transmitted in any form or by any means—electronic, mechanical, photocopy, recording, or any other—except for brief quotations in printed reviews, without the prior written permission of the author.

This is a work of fiction. All incidents and dialogue, other than well-documented historical events, are products of the author's imagination and are not to be construed as real. Where real-life historical figures appear, the situations, incidents, and dialogues concerning those persons are entirely fictional and are not intended to depict actual events or to change the entirely fictional nature of the work.

Published by

3705 Shore Drive
Virginia Beach, VA 23455
800-435-4811
www.koehlerbooks.com

STRONG VINCENT

A CALL TO GLORY

JOHN HINMAN

VIRGINIA BEACH
CAPE CHARLES

CHRISTMAS
—— 1850 ——

Strong Vincent was thirteen years old. Tall for his age and solidly built, he was brought up to respect two things—work and religion. He had chores to do every day, and every night there was allotted time for prayer and for reading the Bible.

On that Christmas Day, Strong's chore was to bundle up his three-year-old sister, Rose, and his five-year-old brother, Boyd. They were traveling to their grandfather John Vincent's house in Waterford, Pennsylvania, which was a twelve-mile ride from their home in Erie. While Strong took care of the younger children, his mother dressed Strong's eight-year-old sister, Belle, who always needed extra help because she was sickly.

"Now, I don't want you two complaining about when dinner will be ready. Do you understand?" Strong admonished his brother and sister.

"But we get our Christmas present at dinnertime. It's hard to wait," Boyd complained.

"Will you take us to see Grandpa's barn?" Rose asked. She, like all of Strong's siblings, loved to visit the animals, especially Grandpa John's horses.

"You can come with me when I take our horses back to the stable when we get to Grandpa's house, but we can't stay very long."

When the carriage was ready, Strong helped his brother and sister to climb aboard. In charge of the carriage was Strong's father, Bethuel B. Vincent, who normally went by his initials. Born in Waterford, BB had moved the family to Erie when he bought into an iron foundry business with the help of his father-in-law, Martin Strong. His first residence in Erie was a house that he rented from Martin Strong. Later he moved his family to their present location on Ninth and Peach Streets.

"Huddle tight. It's cold out here today," BB told his children. A light snow was beginning to fall.

When they finally made it to Waterford, they rode through its streets. Waterford was a small town of about five hundred residents, most of whom lived on farms in the surrounding area. On the main street, there were small businesses and a few houses. At the far end of town was a large brick building, the Eagle Hotel. John Vincent's dwelling, located at the corner of East First Street and Cherry Street, was one of the oldest homes in Waterford. One of the village's earliest settlers, he had brought law and order to the community, and was rewarded by being named the town's judge. Next to the substantial main residence was a series of buildings for storage and holding his carriage. In the back were barns for farming equipment, cattle, and horses. However, while Judge Vincent was a farmer, he made his wealth running a freight business, taking goods from Waterford to Erie and back. Judge Vincent was one of the wealthiest residents of Waterford. He wasn't afraid to share his wealth, making large donations to the church and to township projects.

As BB pulled up to the house, he turned to Strong. "Make sure you put a blanket on the horses. It's colder here than it was in Erie."

"Yes, sir," Strong answered. "Can Rose and Boyd come back, too? I promise we won't be long."

"See to it that you aren't. Your grandfather and grandmother are waiting to see all of you."

Strong unhitched the horses and then walked them back to the barns, slowly thanks to the newly fallen snow. Rose ran ahead so that she could get to the barn first. John Vincent's horse barn provided stalls for all of his horses, and Rose ran to pet each one. Strong found an empty stall and placed both horses in it. He also found blankets for them and then made sure that they had hay and water.

"There, Cody and Ranger. You need to rest up before we make the trip back home. I hope the blankets keep you warm," Strong said.

Rose and Boyd ran around, trying to pet each horse.

"I love this one, Strong," Rose exclaimed.

"That's Buck. He sure is a pretty one."

"Belle is my favorite," Boyd said as he petted the horse's forehead.

"Here, I snuck a carrot for both of you from home. Make sure that you don't let your horse bite off your fingers feeding it to them," Strong told the two. "I miss riding horses with Grandpa. I think that I'll ask him to take me riding this summer. When you're done feeding the horses, we better head up to the house."

When the two children finished feeding the horses their carrots, Strong led them up to the house where they were met by their grandparents with big smiles.

"Hello, Grandma and Grandpa," Rose yelled excitedly. "Merry Christmas!"

"Well, you three finally made it up to the house!" Grandma Nancy said. "Strong, look how you've grown," she said as she gave hugs to all of the children.

After everyone had taken off their coats, Grandma Nancy gave each child a cup of hot chocolate to warm them up. She was in her midsixties, but she was a strong country wife. She did a lot of the chores around the farm and kept the house immaculately clean. She loved spoiling her grandchildren when they came to visit.

After drinking his cocoa, Strong went into the living room to see his grandfather. John Vincent was a large man, standing over six feet tall. He was solidly built from working hard his whole life. Like his wife, John loved to pamper his grandchildren.

"Grandpa, can I come up here for a week after the school year is over?" Strong asked. "I don't get much of a chance to ride horses back in Erie. I used to be pretty good in the saddle, but I am losing my touch. You think me and you can go riding?"

"Why, sure," Grandpa John said. "We haven't gone riding together in a couple of years."

"Can we come?" Rose and Boyd pleaded.

"I'll bring you here," Strong said, "but I'm the only one to go riding with Grandpa."

"Don't worry, Strong, we'll have plenty of time to go off on our own—just the two of us."

The Vincent house was decorated for the holiday season. Candles were everywhere, and elaborate swags made from pine-tree branches graced the living room. At the fireplace were stockings, each holding a piece of candy for the children. The heat of the fire washed away the last remnants of the cold walk from the barn.

"Mom, the house looks terrific. It reminds me of Christmas when I was young," BB said. "I can remember cutting down the tree branches so that you could make decorations with them."

The aroma of Grandma Nancy's pumpkin pie filled the house, causing Rose to ask, "Is it dinnertime yet, Grandpa? I'm hungry." This caused Strong to frown.

"It's almost ready, Rose. Be patient," Grandpa John said. "Did you pet all of my horses when you were out at the barn?"

"I love them all!" she said.

Grandpa John turned to his son. "You know, BB, the thing I miss the most since you moved is seeing your children running around my barn."

"I know, Dad, but my foundry is in Erie, and it's too far to go back and forth every day. You can always come to Erie and see them," BB said.

"I know, but it's not the same."

"We're gonna visit Grandpa for a whole week after school lets out for the summer," Strong told his father. "We're gonna go riding together, ain't we, Grandpa?"

"We sure are," Grandpa John said. "I can't wait."

All of a sudden, Grandma Nancy yelled out, "Dinner is ready!"

The children ran to the dining room and took their seats, waiting anxiously for the grown-ups to sit down.

When everyone was at the table, Grandpa John finally announced, "All right, lift up your plates!"

The children eagerly complied, and each found a crisp new one-hundred-dollar bill under them. After BB moved his family to Erie, John Vincent had created a family tradition of placing money under the children's dinner plates as their Christmas presents.

"Dad, I keep telling you, one hundred dollars is too much to give my children," BB said.

"And every year I tell you that a grandfather's job is to spoil his grandchildren," Grandpa John replied with a wry smile.

After dinner, everyone congregated in the living room, where they sang Christmas carols. To everyone's delight, Strong's mother sang "Silent Night."

"Mom, you have the most beautiful voice. Sing another one for us," Strong said. Sarah Vincent complied with her son's wishes and sang, "Joy to the World."

Afterward, BB read aloud "A Visit from Saint Nicholas" (the original title of "'Twas the Night Before Christmas"). He had an illustrated copy, and Belle and Rose especially liked looking at the pictures. After BB read the poem, everyone got ready to leave.

"Strong, go bring our horses back up and tie them to the carriage. Your mother and I will dress the children. Be careful, because I think we got a lot of snow since we arrived here," BB ordered.

"Yes, sir, I'll be careful. I think we must've gotten two or three inches since we got here. Cody will be anxious. He doesn't like to pull the carriage through the drifts."

It was a dark and cold ride back to Erie. Everyone huddled together to stay warm. All Strong could think about was coming back in May and riding horses with his grandfather.

LAST DAY OF SCHOOL
—— 1851 ——

The greatest day of the school year was always the last day. Strong's classmates ran around at recess, enjoying their classmates one last time; since many students came from farms located miles from school, this was the last chance to be together until the fall.

Erie Academy was a one-room schoolhouse. In 1851, school was not mandatory, and it was not free. BB Vincent paid for Boyd and Strong to attend, firm in his belief that education was important. Students sat in rows, with the oldest students in the rear. As two of the oldest and biggest students in the school, Strong and his buddy Zack McAllister sat in the last row. Zack was as tall as Strong, and solidly built thanks to the hours he spent helping on his father's farm.

At noontime recess, the kids who lived close to the school could walk home for lunch, and the students who traveled farther brought a pail filled with food and ate on the schoolyard lawn. Strong always brought his lunch to eat with Zack because he knew it was too far for Zack to walk home for lunch. The two sat together on the schoolhouse steps.

"So, is this it for you?" Strong asked.

"Yeah, my dad said I will stay on the farm with him in the fall."

In the 1800s, many of the boys ended their academic careers after eighth grade since they were needed on the farm to help with the plowing and planting of crops.

"What about you?" Zack said. "Have you talked to your father yet?"

"No. I'm worried how he will react."

Since the Vincents did not own a farm, Strong's father wanted him to stay in school and one day go to college. But Strong wanted to follow Zack's example and end his schooling. He didn't care much for school, and without Zack in class he knew that he would like it even less.

"Do ya think he'll get really mad?" Zack asked.

"I don't care if he does. I plan to tell him that I'm not going back to school and that is that."

The two boys looked across the schoolyard and saw little Randall Jacobs eating his lunch. He was only a year younger than the two boys, but he was much smaller. He was so small that bigger kids constantly picked on him and stole his lunch pail. One of those bullies was named Michael Reynolds. He had walked over to Randall, intent on taking his lunch. He reached down and grabbed Randall's pail.

"I'll be right back," Strong said.

Strong was bigger than Michael, and he walked over and looked Michael in the eyes.

"Give it back," he snarled.

Michael handed the pail back to Randall. "Sorry, kid. I didn't bring anything to eat." As soon as Randall took back his lunch, Michael ran away.

"Thanks, Strong," Randall said.

"Listen, Randall. You have to do something about growing over the summer. I can't keep chasing students away when they come to take your lunch from you."

"My dad says the same thing, since I'm too small to work on the farm with him. I wish that I could take a pill or something to grow."

As Strong walked back to where Zack was eating, Boyd Vincent went over to eat lunch with Randall. No one would bother them for fear of facing Strong.

"Why do you always help out that runt?" Zack asked as Strong sat back down.

"He's not so bad, and it's not fair that others take advantage of him because he's so small. I don't know what's gonna happen to him next year when I'm not here."

Zack smiled. "You think you won't be here, but you still haven't told your father."

"I'm not coming back. I'll bet you money I'm not coming back."

After school let out, Strong and Boyd walked home, accompanied by the two Reed children who lived next door. Robert Reed was a year older than Strong, and Sarah Reed was a year younger.

"Have you talked to your father yet?" Robert asked.

Boyd butted in. "What are you gonna talk to Dad about?"

"That's none of your business, Boyd. Why don't you and Sarah race home and leave us alone?"

"Come on, Sarah. I'll race ya."

Boyd and Sarah ran ahead.

"I'm gonna tell him tonight," Strong said. "If you hear a lot of screaming, you'll know the cause of it."

When Strong got home, his mother called for him to come into the kitchen.

"Strong, have a cookie and some milk. Boyd told me how you helped Randall at school today."

"He's so small, Mom. It ain't right for others to take advantage of him."

"You know, when you were born, I let your father come up with a name for you. Your Grandpa Martin had helped him so much in business, and he wanted to reward him by naming you after your grandfather. I thought he was going to call you Martin, but instead he wanted to call you Strong, your grandfather's last name. I was worried others might pick on you, make you prove your name, but your father said that you would grow into it, and you sure did. I'm happy that instead of using your size to bully others, you use it to protect them. I'm so proud of you."

"Thanks, Mom. I didn't really do anything. I just looked at the kid and he ran away." Strong sat at the table and ate his cookie. He thought of what he had planned to do later in the evening and wanted his mother's advice as to the timing of the conversation. "Mom, I want to talk to Dad about something important. Do you think I should wait until after dinner?"

"You know your father wants dinner on the table the second he walks through that door at six o'clock. Better talk to him after supper."

During dinner, Strong pushed his food around the plate. His mother had made a nice meal of chicken and biscuits, but Strong only took a few bites of it. His father made a few comments about not wasting good food, but when it was time to clear the table, Strong still had eaten very little.

"Dad, can I talk to you in the study?" Strong asked nervously.

"You and Boyd have to take care of the dishes. Then we can sit down and talk," his father answered.

Seeing that her son was troubled, his mother said, "I'll help Boyd tonight. You two go right ahead and have your talk."

The study was BB's office. It was filled with books, and his desk had all sorts of papers strewn across it, as BB did a lot of the company's paperwork at home.

As he sat behind the desk, BB gave Strong a stern look, unhappy that his son had skipped his nightly chore. Strong swallowed hard, knowing that this was going to be an upsetting discussion. He had to find the courage to defend his decision.

"So, what is so important that you avoided your chores?" BB growled.

"Dad, today was the last day of the school year. In the fall, I don't want to go back."

"You want to quit school? Why do you think that I would stand for that?" BB looked even angrier than before.

Strong wanted to stand his ground. He knew that if he gave in, he would be going back to school. "Zack McAllister isn't going back, and I don't want to, either."

"Zack's father needs him on the farm. I don't have a farm, and I want you to continue your education. There's no reason for you not to go back."

"But Dad, I know everything the teacher's teaching, and I don't want to go to college. I'm perfectly happy doing other things."

"No son of mine is going to quit school and be lazy around the house. You want to quit school? Then you will come work for me in the foundry starting Monday. One day you'll have to run it, so you might as well learn it from the bottom up."

This was not what Strong expected. He thought he'd have to work around the house, but he never thought his dad would make him work in the foundry. He searched quickly for a way out.

"Remember Grandpa John said that I could go out there for a week and ride horses? Can I still do that?"

BB was disappointed in his son's insistence on not going back to school. The problem was that if he also forbade Strong from going to visit his grandfather, he would have a whole lot of new problems.

Feeling that there was no good way out of the situation, BB said, "All right you can go, but after one week, I will become your teacher and the foundry will be your school."

"But I won't turn fourteen until next month. What if I can't do all the things your workers do?"

"This is the deal—you work at my foundry, or you go to school. If you find the work is too hard, then you go back to school in the fall."

It was Strong's turn to feel trapped, and he reluctantly replied, "Okay, I'll work in the foundry. You won't have to worry about me returning to school, because I won't give up."

"Fine. Enjoy your week at your grandfather's house, because after that you're my employee."

Neither adversary was happy as Strong got up to leave the room. Strong got his wish about not going back to school, but what he didn't know was what that victory would cost him.

GRANDPA'S HOUSE
—— 1851 ——

Strong Vincent took Boyd and Rose to his Grandfather John's house after church on Sunday. He thought about his two goals as he drove the carriage to Waterford: one was to learn better horsemanship, and the second was to get his grandfather to side with him against working at the foundry. He knew Grandpa John would take his side.

Strong helped Rose and Boyd get packed before leaving to travel to their grandparents' house. BB took Strong aside to talk to him.

"Strong, remember after this week at your grandfather's house, you start to work for me next week."

"I know, Dad. I still think that I am too young to work at the foundry."

"That's our deal. You can back out at any time. Just promise to go back to school."

Strong drove the carriage out to their grandparents' house. Grandpa John and Grandma Nancy were happy to see the children. Rose and Boyd ran down to see the horses as soon as they arrived.

On Monday morning, Strong and Grandpa John went out riding. Strong's grandfather was widely considered to be the best horseman around, and he began by telling Strong that riding a horse was more than just jumping on and telling the horse to go. The first part of riding was to look ahead and get a good idea of the terrain. This helped determine how fast to run the horse. He also taught Strong how to slow down as they left a clearing and headed into the woods. That way, if there was an obstacle such as a creek ahead, he could see it in plenty of time to help the horse to cross it. Little did Strong know that everything his grandfather was teaching him would come in handy as an officer in the Union army later in his life.

When they came up to a wide field of short grass, Grandpa John slowed the horses to a trot to give them a little rest. Strong saw his chance.

"Grandpa, I'll be fourteen in a couple of weeks, and I think I am too old to go back to school. I pretty much know everything the teacher is teaching."

"Did you talk to your father about this?" Grandpa John asked.

"Yeah, but he said that if I wasn't going back to school, I had to go to work in the foundry. Grandpa, I've been in the foundry a bunch of times, but I have never seen a boy my age working there."

"I think your father is afraid that you'll sit around all day and do nothing. Maybe that's why he wants you to work."

"But aren't you afraid I could get hurt in such a dangerous place?"

"You're right about that. The foundry is no place for fun and games. You'll have to pay attention to the other workers and do as they say. What happens if the work is too hard for you?"

"Then I go back to school," Strong lamented. "I don't want to go back to school. My friend Zack isn't going back, either."

"What does Zack's father do?"

"He's a farmer. We don't own a farm, or I'd be happy to work it."

"I get it now," Grandpa Vincent said. "You want me to pressure my son to not send you to work in the foundry but still let you quit school. Strong, I have never come between my son and how he disciplines his family, especially because in this case I think he is right. If you go to work in the foundry, it is because you chose not to go back to school. You're a big boy now. Your choices carry consequences. It's not my job to stand in between them."

Strong felt downhearted as he saw his big plan fall apart. He had been so sure that he could count on his grandfather's backing. Now he was back to having to choose.

"Come on, Strong, don't look so glum. Let's race the horses back home." Then Grandpa John spurred the horse and the two of them galloped away.

After dinner, Strong went to bed discouraged; he had to think of something to convince his father to not make him work in the foundry. Then it came to him. Starting on Wednesday, he, Boyd, and Rose would be spending a couple of days at Grandpa Martin's house. They also lived in Waterford. Grandpa John took his father's side because BB was his son. But BB was not Grandpa Martin's son. Grandpa Martin would never let Strong risk injury by having to work in the foundry at age thirteen.

He couldn't wait for Wednesday.

After two days, the three Vincent children walked through Waterford to Martin Strong's farm. Like John Vincent, Martin was an early settler and had taken up farming and acquiring land. By the time Strong came to visit, Martin Strong had added over eight hundred acres to his farm and was far and away the area's largest landowner.

Martin had a big house, but he also had barns for the horses and cattle, a dairy barn for milking the cows, a wood house, a cider press, and a slaughterhouse. Martin Strong also made his own syrup in a small shack. It was almost like he had his own little village. Strong, Boyd, and Rose loved running from building to building, but the best thing about visiting their grandparents was that Grandma Sarah always fed them big slices of freshly baked bread covered in butter and maple syrup.

Since Martin Strong had once enlisted in the state militia, the locals referred to him as Captain Strong. A deeply religious man, he had also allowed the Union Church to be built on his farmland. Most of Waterford could be found there on Sunday mornings.

As the three Vincents came through the door, Grandma Sarah was waiting with their favorite treat. After they had each devoured their slice of bread, Boyd and Rose wanted to check out the various buildings. Strong told them to go on ahead—he wanted to talk with Grandpa Martin.

After the two of them left, Strong immediately went into his sob story about having to work in the foundry.

"Now, Strong," Martin told him, "I know your father was hoping that you would go on to college. He wants you to come back and use your knowledge to help make the foundry run more efficiently."

"But he's the one who wants me to go to college," Strong cried. "I really don't care to."

"Remember, you are the oldest boy. With that comes responsibility. You talked about how your friend Zack is working on the farm. Is he the oldest in his family?"

"Yeah."

"Well, his father is doing for him what your father wants to do for you. Zack will be learning how to run the farm for when his father is too old to do it. Your father wants you to learn the foundry. Knowing the business from the bottom up will help you make changes later so that the foundry will be more productive."

"But, Grandpa, I could get hurt really bad."

"Yes, you could. That's why you have to listen to the workers and do everything they say."

"Don't you think I should wait a couple of years at least?"

"Perhaps. But if you are waiting, you have to go back to school." Strong started to protest, but his grandfather cut him off with a look. "Your father has given you a fair choice. I'm sure that if the work is truly too dangerous, your father has partners who will speak up. The Himrod brothers, for example."

Strong had struck out with both grandfathers. It was now his choice whether to go back to school or work. And he did not want to go back to school.

Strong stayed at Grandpa Vincent's house so long on Sunday that by the time he returned to Erie with Boyd and Rose, it was already dark. He hoped his father would give him Monday off because of the late hour, and he did.

That was the only part of his plan that worked.

On Tuesday he would become the newest employee of Vincent, Himrod, & Co.

VINCENT, HIMROD, & CO.
—— 1851 ——

B. B. Vincent, William Himrod, David Himrod, and William Johnson bought an iron foundry located on the corner of Twelfth and French Streets of Erie, Pennsylvania in 1840. The original name was the Presque Isle Foundry, but after the purchase they changed it to honor the founding partners. In late 1851, the same year Strong Vincent started working in the foundry, the partners changed the name again to Erie City Iron Works.

The company specialized in making boilers, engines, and machinery used in sawmills, then later expanded to include railroad cars. Over the years, the Erie City Iron Works became one of the largest producers of boilers and engines in the entire United States.

On the Tuesday Strong Vincent was supposed to start working, BB got to the foundry early so he could speak to the foreman, Benjamin Coates, who had been with Vincent, Himrod, & Co. since it had first opened.

"I have a favor to ask," BB said. "My son, Strong, starts working today. I don't want you or anyone else to take it easy on him. Start him off in the furnace room and make sure you make it tough."

"Why? Isn't he a little young?"

"He's thirteen, but he'll be fourteen in a couple of weeks. I want him to stay in school, but he's got it in his head that he knows it all. I'm hoping a few days of real work will have him running back to school."

When Strong showed up, he reported to Benjamin, and the two

toured the furnace area where Strong would be working.

"The first thing you have to do every day is put on these protective shoes," Coates instructed. "You'll be working around a furnace that is over two thousand degrees. You keep them street shoes on and you'll burn your feet. Got it? And put on this protective apron, too."

"Yes sir," Strong said, wanting to show his father he could be a good worker.

"The furnace has to be constantly fed. You fall behind doing that and all production suffers. Now come over here to where we keep the iron ore." Strong followed Benjamin around the plant. "The furnace needs four hundred pounds of iron ore every half hour. It also needs fifteen bushels of charcoal to keep the flame going. Your job is to work with these guys over there to feed the furnace. Don't let them boss you around, but don't slack off, either."

Three older men were standing by the pile of iron ore, looking at Strong.

"The older gentleman is Steve Rackowski, next to him is Denny Wilhelm, and the guy on the end is David Leonard," Benjamin told Strong. "You listen to those guys. They've been working here for a long time. Hey, you guys! This is Strong Vincent. He's gonna be working with you now. Steve, I want you to train him in feeding the furnace."

With that, Benjamin Coates walked away to check on other areas of the foundry.

David snarled, "Is your old man one of the owners? Did he send you down here to spy on us?"

"My dad is one of the owners, but he is only making me work down here because I told him I didn't want to go back to school in the fall," Strong said nervously.

"Well, kid," Steve said, "I wasn't much for schoolin' myself. Now pick up that shovel and start loading up iron ore in that wheelbarrow. The furnace is hungry."

Strong struggled to fill up his wheelbarrow with the heavy pieces of ore. The three older workers laughed as they watched.

"Is the work too hard for you, little boy?" David teased. Strong ignored him.

Every half hour, the furnace had to be fed to keep it hot enough to melt the iron ore. Strong silently loaded his wheelbarrow, rolled it up to the top of the furnace, and dumped its contents down into the belly. By mid-morning, he seemed to have earned Steve's respect.

"Hey, kid," Steve called. "Come up here with me." The two walked up closer to the furnace. "Do you feel that heat?"

"Yes, sir. It's like it could burn my face off," Strong answered.

"We don't have a thermometer that registers over two thousand degrees, so you need to get a sense of the right temperature over time. If it's not as hot as it is now, the molders can't make the products, and we get yelled at. So, you gotta come up here and stand as close as you can to make sure."

"How long does it take to learn how to feel the right temperature on your face?"

"Won't take you long, kid. Come up here every time you see me heading up without a load."

"Yes, sir," Strong said as he went down to begin loading another wheelbarrow with iron ore.

At lunchtime, Strong sat by himself, since Steve, Denny, and David were telling stories and jokes full of bad words Strong could never repeat around the dinner table. He was tired, but he was beginning to like Steve, who was always patient with him. Denny was also helpful, but David was mean and wanted nothing to do with him.

The rest of the day seemed to take forever. Strong always tried to be the first to fill his wheelbarrow and head up the path to the furnace. His muscles screamed in pain, but he would never let the other three know it. Finally, at the end of the day, Steve and Denny gathered around him.

"You did all right, kid," Steve said. "I didn't think you had a full day's work in you, but you proved me wrong."

"Yeah, you did okay, kid," Denny added. "How do you feel?"

"More tired than I've ever been in my life," Strong said.

Steve and Denny laughed.

"Just wait 'til the morning," Steve said. "Every muscle in your whole body will ache. I tell ya what. We'll take it easy on you tomorrow. We all know what that feeling is like after the first day on the job."

"Why doesn't David like me?" Strong asked.

"Oh, he hates everybody. He has a chip on his shoulder the size of State Street," Denny said. "Don't let him bother you."

"C'mon, kid," Steve said. "Let's go wash off all that black dust. You can't go home looking like that."

"Steve, can I ask you a favor? My name is Strong. Can you call me that instead of 'kid' tomorrow?"

Steve respected the request and thought that Strong deserved to be treated like an adult if he was working as hard as one. "I'll make you a deal. I'll stop calling you 'kid' if you stop calling me 'sir.' Every time you call me that I think my father is around somewhere."

When Strong got home, he immediately flopped into a chair, totally exhausted. Rose and Belle came over to play a game, but he was too tired to join in. At dinner, he almost fell face-forward into his dinner plate.

"Bethuel, look at Strong!" his mother cried. "You can't have him coming home like this. He's just a boy."

"He can quit any time he wants," BB answered. "He can go back to school and forget all about the foundry."

Strong sat up straight. "I'm just tired from my first day," he said. "I'll get used to the job."

And the battle was on. Strong was determined to keep working. BB was determined to make his job no easy task.

At the end of the first week, BB went over to Benjamin Coates to get a rundown of Strong's performance.

"So, how's my boy doing?"

"I know you want him to quit and go back to school, Mr. Vincent, but I have to say that your boy is one of my best workers. Who would've thought a thirteen-year-old could hold up so well down here? He works harder than some of the men who've been here for years. 'Strong' sure is an appropriate name for him."

"I don't know whether to be proud or disappointed," BB said. "He came home exhausted after that first day, but every day since he's come home smiling and wrestling around with the other kids. Let's keep him loading the furnace for a while, and then we'll see what else we can have him do."

Strong loaded the furnace for three months before BB transferred him to the area where the molten iron was molded into products. Strong was sad to say goodbye to Steve and Denny, but he was excited to learn a new job.

"You have to be really careful here," Benjamin Coates told him. "The iron ore comes out in the cast house as a hot liquid ready to be molded. Vincent, Himrod, & Co. is especially known for producing boilers and engines." He walked over to one of the molders. "Barry, this is Strong Vincent. He's here to learn from you. Teach him the right method of casting."

Barry Johnson was the company's best molder, his high output equaling a high amount of money. But now, having to teach Strong Vincent the trade, he was worried his own production would fall off as well as his earnings.

"Come here, kid. In this job, you gotta work fast but you also gotta work safely. You let any of that molten iron get on you and it'll burn your skin right off. You do what I say when I say it. I ain't takin' a pay cut because I got a daddy's boy to train. You got that?"

"Yes, sir, Mr. Johnson. You tell me what to do, and I'll get it done."

"We take the molten iron and run it into different molds. Some of the other guys make parts for engines, but I just do boilers. Don't slow me down, kid, or I'll get mad. Now let's get to work."

The work of the molder was hard and hot. First, Barry made Strong watch him pour the liquid ore into the boiler molds. After a while,

Barry let Strong help, and the two of them made more boilers working together than Barry had ever made in one day. From that point, Barry treated Strong with more respect.

Strong worked with the molders for over a year, becoming an expert molder second only to Barry himself.

In 1853, Strong's father moved him upstairs to the administrative offices, where BB soon understood that Strong had been right: his son had learned enough in school to be a part of the working world. Strong started off by keeping track of the company's accounting books. Later he ordered all of the supplies. As the company grew and prospered, part of its success was due to Strong's expert administrative work.

By 1854, when Strong was seventeen years old, he was practically running the entire operation. He knew everything there was to know about running a foundry, from producing a product to being in charge of its workers. But Strong started thinking that he wanted more out of his life. He remembered how his father was originally against him quitting school and going to work, but Strong began to think that maybe his father was right about what he wanted to do to help him succeed in life. He was ready to follow his father's wishes.

Strong Vincent wanted to go to college.

COLLEGE DAYS
—— 1854–1859 ——

Strong was excited to tell his father that he was finally getting his wish for him to go to college. After speaking with some of the local businessmen, BB ultimately decided on sending his son to Trinity College in Hartford, Connecticut. The college was known for its liberal arts education and its cultivation of a student's independent thinking. The cost might be a little high, but according to B. B. Vincent, a good education was worth it.

BB's main concern was that Strong had ended his schooling after eighth grade and would have to work hard to catch up to the knowledge of the other students. Strong assured his father that because he had taught him the value of hard work, he was prepared to study hard in order to do well in college.

BB accompanied his son on the train to Hartford. This was the first time Strong would be living away from his family, and his father wanted to help him get settled.

When they reached the campus, the college buildings impressed both father and son. There were two main buildings—one for classes, and the other a dormitory that housed the small number of students. Rising with grandeur, the two buildings were brick, with pointed peaks at the top. The campus was lined with trees, which added to its impressiveness.

Strong and his father went to speak with the president of the college, Daniel Goodwin. BB explained how Strong left school after eighth grade but was able to run his company three years later. There was a little hesitancy on Goodwin's part to accept Strong, but he decided to enroll him in the school.

After the conversation, BB said, "Let's go up to your dorm room and get you situated."

At Trinity, students resided one per room. Strong's room was small, holding only a bed, a desk, and a dresser. One luxury it had, however, was a fireplace for cold nights.

"I barely fit into this place," Strong said.

"It's got a bed for sleeping and a desk for studying. That's all you're going to need. Let's walk around the grounds."

As the two exited the room, they met the student next door, Oliver Woodward. Smaller than Strong, he seemed scholarly, dressed in an expensive suit. The three introduced themselves.

"Are you from around here?" Oliver asked.

"No, we're from Pennsylvania. How about you?" Strong responded.

"I've lived in Hartford my whole life. I studied in London, England, for a few months last year, but I came back to go to college at Trinity. My father went here years ago."

"You see, Strong? You have a nice classmate right next door. I think you will be all right," BB said.

"It was sure nice meeting you, Strong. I look forward to seeing you in classes. I'm sorry, but I have to excuse myself; I am meeting some friends in town for dinner," Oliver said as he hurried down the hallway.

"I have got to get back to Erie, son. Write to me and your mother and let us know how you're doing. Study hard and remember to follow the school's rules."

"Don't worry, Dad. I'll be studying so much, I won't have time to get into trouble."

Incoming Trinity freshmen were required to attend the President's Convocation in the Trinity Chapel on their first day. Strong's first college experience was tough, as a day of speeches almost made him fall asleep. When the speeches were over, there was a matriculation ceremony—a tradition followed ever since the college was founded in 1826. In this ceremony, students were required to sign "The Charter and Standing Rules." After signing his name, Strong agreed to follow the rules of the college, and then he was ready to start his career as a Trinity student.

Strong's freshman year was as difficult as he had expected. He studied every evening, but his grades stayed in the average to a little above average range. Still, Strong made friends easily. He was tall and good-looking and possessed a well-built physique thanks to working in the iron foundry. He also got along well with Oliver. One night, Strong went to Oliver's room to get some help in his math class. The two also got to know each other and share their experiences before coming to college.

"When I was thirteen, I thought I was too smart for education," Strong shared. "Now that I'm here, I don't know if I made the right decision."

"You'll be okay," Oliver said. "It's just going to take time. I'm impressed you were running an entire business at seventeen."

"Thanks. What does your father do?"

"He's one of the most respected lawyers in town. When I graduate, I plan to join him."

"Thanks again for the math help," Strong said, then smiled. "Don't be surprised if I'm back for help often."

One class Strong liked was literature. In it, he read *Uncle Tom's Cabin* by Harriet Beecher Stowe. The novel stirred up emotions in both the northern and southern parts of the United States. It's depicture of slavery as an evil fueled the fire of an abolitionist movement looking to ban slavery. Strong had known that slavery existed down south, but he never really had an opinion on it given that he was too busy working full-time in the foundry. But in class, he read about Uncle Tom being forced to live his life enslaved. Later, he was sold to a man named Simon Legree, who had Tom beaten to death when he tried to help another slave. After reading the novel, Strong's views on slavery changed—he decided the institution of slavery was a great offense. Some of his classmates were abolitionists, meaning they wanted to abolish slavery right away; Strong wanted to end slavery, but he was hoping that a solution could come through Congress.

In the spring of 1855, Strong's first year of college came to a merciful end. He welcomed his return home to Erie.

In his sophomore year, Strong still studied hard, but he had more chances to go into town with friends. One evening, Oliver, Strong, and another classmate decided to dine at one of the restaurants near the city's riverfront. As they strolled down the main avenue, the students spotted a trio of young ladies.

"Good evening, Ladies," Oliver said gallantly.

The three girls giggled, but Strong noticed that one of them was particularly attractive. He went over to talk to her.

"It's a beautiful evening. Are you three in town for dinner? We would love for you to join us."

"No, we're here to pick up some supplies to take back to Farmington," the girl said shyly.

"My name is Strong Vincent. I'm a student at Trinity College."

"Strong. Is that a nickname?"

"No, that's my given name. I'm named after my grandfather. Strong is his last name. How about you? What's your name?"

"Elizabeth Carter. I'm a teacher at Miss Porter's School in Farmington."

"Well," said Strong, "if my grade-school teacher was as pretty as you, I would have stayed in school a lot longer."

"Thank you, Strong," Elizabeth said as she blushed. Then she turned to her companions. "Girls, we have to be getting back to school before Miss Porter worries."

The girls looked disappointed, but dutifully turned to walk away. They headed toward a wagon loaded with supplies for the school. Strong rushed over to talk to Elizabeth before she left.

"Do you think that I could call on you at your school? I would love to see you again."

Elizabeth blushed. "I guess you can try. It's up to Miss Porter."

"Well, tell Miss Porter that this big, handsome, but respectful boy would like to spend time with you. She can even chaperone," Strong said with a sly grin.

The next weekend, Strong rented a horse from a stable in town and rode to Farmington, about ten miles from Hartford. Sarah Porter had opened her school so that young women could receive a quality education. Located on a main street, the building contained both schoolrooms and living quarters.

Summoning his courage, Strong knocked on the front door. Miss Sarah Porter met him. In her midforties, she had a very dignified appearance. Her dark hair was pulled back in a bun, and she was wearing a long, plain-looking black dress with a white collar.

Miss Porter took a few seconds to examine him.

"Are you this Strong Vincent that Elizabeth has been talking about?" she finally asked, curtly enough that Strong wanted to run back to his horse and make a quick getaway.

"Yes, ma'am," was all Strong could say in response.

"Well, I do not like gentleman callers disrupting the girls' schedule, but Elizabeth said you were a fine young man. You and Elizabeth can sit out here on the front porch and talk, and I will send one of the girls out with refreshments."

"Thank you, Miss Porter, and may I say that you have a fine-looking residence and school building here," Strong said, trying to get on Miss Porter's good side.

Miss Porter only gave Strong a sharp look.

Elizabeth came to the door, and Strong was relieved when Miss Porter started to make her way back inside.

"Do not be out here too long, is that understood?" Miss Porter warned Elizabeth.

"We won't. Strong has to ride back to Hartford tonight." She waited for Miss Porter to go inside and then said to Strong, "Sorry. Miss Porter sounds a little rough, but she really cares for all of the young women here."

"That's okay. I suppose my mother would act in much the same way if a boy called on one of my sisters. Have you been at the school long?"

"My mother died when I was young, and I don't know where my father is, so I grew up with my older sister and her husband in New Jersey. That's where I met Miss Porter, who took me under her wing. She enrolled me in her school, and when I graduated, Miss Porter kept me on as a teacher. I really owe a lot to her."

"That was really nice of Miss Porter, to take you in and help you. I was taken aback from her stern appearance, but now I see that there is a softer side to her."

A young girl came out with a pitcher of lemonade and two glasses. She giggled at seeing a grown man sitting on the front porch, but Elizabeth gave her a stern look that kindly suggested she should go back inside.

Strong told Elizabeth how he quit school at age thirteen, and how his father made him work in his iron foundry. He described how he started with the most menial job and worked up to almost running the entire company by himself in just a couple of years.

"Your father must've been so proud of you running his company at such a young age," Lizzie said. Lizzie was her less formal name that she preferred to be called.

"Yeah, but I think he respected me more with my decision to go to college. It was always his dream that I attend a college, and when I told him of my intentions, he was really proud of me."

"I often wonder what happened to my father and if he would be proud of what I am doing as a school teacher. You're lucky to have both of your parents that have helped mold you into a fine, young man."

As Strong talked to Lizzie, he couldn't help but admire her beauty. She was confident, and she liked what she was doing, helping to teach young women to find that self-assuredness that she possessed. The more that the two talked, the more Strong fell in love with her. After a little time together, Strong knew that one day he would marry Lizzie.

Strong didn't want the evening to end, but after an hour or so, Miss Porter told him that the visit was over. He was, however, welcome to come back and call on Lizzie again. Strong saw this as a humble victory.

With Miss Porter standing right there, Strong's goodbye to Lizzie was only a quick embrace.

As the school year progressed, so did Strong and Lizzie's relationship. Strong rode to Farmington as often as he could. Sometimes they were even able to meet in Hartford. His love for her grew stronger on every visit. The one holdup was Strong's studies—it was hard juggling schoolwork and time to be with Lizzie. His grades were improving, but he was still far from the head of his class.

One evening, after studying hard for a few hours, Strong decided to take a walk to clear his mind. He saw a group of four classmates talking to a much larger guy he recognized as one of Trinity's security guards.

"Hey, Strong," one of the classmates called. "Do you know Ken? He works at the college. He's filling us in on the local girls and who to stay away from."

Ken had the air of someone who thought he was better than everybody else. As soon as the guard opened his mouth, Strong knew his first impression was right.

Ken described one of the girls from town in the most disparaging way and then said terrible things about her behavior. He said that the girl wore plain clothes and her long hair could not hide her big nose. Then he said that she was the kind of girl that had loose morals, especially in encouraging men. Then Ken changed the topic to attack a different girl, making similar remarks. Strong realized that the woman he was now talking about was Lizzie, His vision turned red.

"That's my girl, Elizabeth Carter. I will give you one chance to take back what you said and apologize."

"Whatcha gonna do, college boy? It's not my fault you like that harlot," Ken said with a laugh and took a step toward Strong.

"You take it back and apologize, or I'll make you take it back," Strong growled.

The four classmates retreated a few steps, leaving Strong and Ken in the middle by themselves.

"Go ahead, college boy," Ken said, snickering. "I tell you what—just to give you a sporting chance, I'll even let you have the first punch, but then I'm gonna beat you bad."

The anger in Strong boiled. Losing his temper, Strong let loose with a wicked punch that caught Ken square in the face. Ken's knees buckled and he fell to the ground. Strong jumped on him and began pummeling him with punch after punch. It took all of the four classmates' strength to finally pry Strong off of Ken. The big guy lay on the ground, badly beaten.

"You better get outta here right now," one of the classmates said. "We'll take Ken to get medical help, but you have to get out of here fast."

It took a while before Strong finally calmed down enough to think about the consequences of his actions. He had never lost his temper like that before. He needed to see Lizzie and talk things over.

He made it to Farmington at a later hour than usual, but Miss Porter allowed Lizzie to talk to him for a few minutes. Strong told her about what had happened.

"Strong, those were just words. They can't hurt me. I know that Ken. I don't like him, but you beating him up puts you in a lot of trouble."

"I know, Lizzie. I only wanted to protect your honor. If he had taken back what he said, I wouldn't be in this mess."

"What do think the college will do? Didn't you have to sign something about your behavior when you first started school?"

"Yeah. I can only guess what the punishment might be. Hopefully, they'll just confine me to my room after classes for a while. I'm pretty much there every day anyway."

"What if they expel you? You'll go back home, and I'll never see you again."

Strong felt bad for risking his relationship over starting the fight. He could see the hurt in her eyes at the thought of never seeing him again.

He said, "Lizzie, I love you. No matter what happens at Trinity, my feelings for you will never change. My dream is that we live every day together. Whatever happens to me at the college will never keep us apart. I'll get a note out to you tomorrow letting you know what my punishment is, but I better head back."

Strong hugged Lizzie and took a long look into her beautiful eyes. Then he made his way back to Trinity, hoping for the best.

In the morning, as Strong was dressing, a school administrator appeared at his door and told him that Mr. Goodwin, the college's president, wanted to see him right away. Strong finished getting ready in a hurry.

It was a bright, sunny day, but you wouldn't have known it inside President Goodwin's office. He had all of the windows covered by heavy drapes. Strong looked around the room and saw numerous bookshelves with hundreds, maybe thousands, of books. He wondered if they were for show or if Goodwin had actually read all of them.

The man himself sat behind the desk. President Goodwin was forty-five years old, but he looked at least twenty years older than that, with a face seemingly chiseled from stone. Strong doubted it had cracked a smile in many years.

"Please have a seat, Master Vincent," Goodwin told Strong coldly. "Do you want to explain what happened in the courtyard yesterday?"

"Your security guard, Ken, was describing the town's young ladies in a rather insulting way. One of the ladies he was describing was a girl I have been seeing, so I asked him to take back what he said. When he wouldn't, we got into a fight."

"I heard it wasn't much of a fight. I heard you knocked him to the ground and beat him severely."

"Yes, I did, sir, and I am sorry, but the things he said about my friend were terrible. Wouldn't you get angry if someone said nasty things about your wife?"

"We are not here to talk about my behavior; we are here to talk about yours. That was not an acceptable response for a Trinity student.

I met with the other administrators this morning, and we all agreed you should be discharged. You are to collect your things and be off this campus by nightfall."

Strong was stunned. He knew that he would be punished, but he didn't think it would be this severe. "You're expelling me? Don't I at least get a second chance to show you that I can follow the rules?"

"The punishment has been decided. When you first came here you signed the charter. There is no talk of second chances in the charter. Now, you need to go to your room and gather your belongings." President Goodwin stood, and Strong knew there was nothing more to say.

After packing his clothes, Strong wrote a short letter to Elizabeth. He again told her that he loved her and promised to continue writing, but he had to catch the train to Erie. He would let her know about his future plans. Then he went to the post office.

It was a long train ride back home to Erie, one Strong spent nervously wondering what to tell his father about the incident.

As he arrived back home and opened the door, his brother and sisters ran to greet him. Hearing the noise, his mother and father came to the front room.

"Did school let out early this year?" his mother asked.

Strong didn't answer, but instead turned to his father. "Dad, can I speak to you in private?"

"Sure, come into the study." BB led his son into the next room and shut the door.

Strong told his father about the whole incident and the punishment he had received from Trinity. Talking about the incident stirred his emotions, and Strong's body began shaking. Trying to remain calm, he apologized to his father for losing his temper.

"You must really like this girl," BB said, trying to calm him.

"I want to marry Lizzie as soon as my life is going in the right direction. You would like her too, Dad. She even got mad at me for defending her reputation with the fight."

"Strong, you can't lose your temper like you did yesterday. When things are bad, that's when you have to remain the calmest. I am proud of you for defending your girlfriend's honor, but I'm disappointed in the way you did it."

"I don't know what happened to me. I lost my temper really bad. And now the big problem is Trinity won't take me back. Do you think another college would accept me?"

"Let me look into things," BB said, clearly relieved that Strong wanted to continue his schooling. "You deserve a little rest after the last couple of days."

BB soon came up with a plan to get his son back to school in the fall.

"Where are we going?" Strong asked his father when they boarded a train several weeks later. BB was keeping the name of the new school a secret.

"We're heading to Cambridge, Massachusetts. I think you'll like this new school. It has a much better reputation than Trinity."

When the two got off the train and made their way to the campus, Strong realized his father was helping him to enroll in Harvard University. If Trinity College had impressed the Vincents, Harvard's campus dazzled them. There were so many big buildings that made up the campus. The cupola of the chapel rose above many of the surrounding buildings.

When they reached the admissions office, BB told Strong, "You stay out here for a little bit, and let me handle the details about getting you enrolled here."

Strong found a chair outside the conference room. He tried to hear what was going on inside, but he could hardly hear anything. A few minutes later, a distinguished-looking gentleman invited Strong inside.

A panel of five administrators was seated around a big table. Strong took a seat next to his father.

"We would like to welcome you to Harvard next fall. The one concession is you must repeat your sophomore year. Do you see any problem with that?"

"Uh, no, sir," Strong blurted. He couldn't believe he was going to be a student at Harvard University.

After talking with the administrators, BB and Strong strolled around the campus.

"Dad, how did you get them to let me enroll here? Did you tell them what happened at Trinity?"

"Yes, and they are happy to put the incident in the past, so long as you don't repeat it."

"Don't worry. I've learned my lesson."

BB never told his son how he got him into Harvard. However, soon after the admissions meeting, several building projects on campus, previously on hold for lack of money, started up again, fully funded.

Harvard was a good fit for Strong Vincent. He became very popular among the students, with friends among freshmen and seniors alike. His popularity led him to be president of a couple of the campus society groups. His grades were about the same as they had been at Trinity, but he built strong relationships with professors in the classroom.

Instead of a scientific education, Strong soon decided he wanted to become a lawyer. Harvard's law school was famous, and Strong worked hard to keep his grades up.

Strong wrote to Elizabeth often. Farmington was about one hundred miles from Cambridge, and so seeing her was almost impossible, but the two kept up their relationship through their letters to each other. In 1858, Strong was able to visit Elizabeth during a break. The two took a long walk through the small town of Farmington, and then they sat on the front porch of Miss Porter's residence and talked about their future.

"Lizzie, I'll be graduating next year. After I begin my career as a lawyer, we can be married. I don't see anything getting in our way."

"Strong, I can't wait to be with you. Sometimes it's hard to be so far away from you. I can't wait to spend the rest of my life seeing you every day."

"Well, that won't be long. There's nothing that can keep us away from spending our life together."

"Strong, I worry about what is going on in Washington between the North and the South. The slavery problem seems to be getting worse. If the president tries to do away with slavery, the southern states will leave the country! What if civil war breaks out?"

"President James Buchanan won't get rid of slavery. He doesn't seem to do very much of anything."

"I worry about our future." Lizzie looked at Strong with sad eyes like she was about to cry.

"We'll be okay, Lizzie," Strong said as he took her into his arms and held her close. "I'm more worried about getting through my senior year than civil war breaking out." The two parted with heavy hearts, still worrying about their future lives together.

In 1859, Strong Vincent was ready to graduate, but before graduation came Harvard's Class Day. Even though Strong was nowhere close to being a top student academically, he was among the leaders socially, which meant he was named a Class Day marshal. The ceremony involved dancing and refreshments, followed by the cheering seniors marching around the grounds.

After graduating at twenty-two, Strong's plans were to return to Erie and become a full-fledged lawyer, then marry Elizabeth. But some of the fears they had expressed about the future of the country began to hinder those plans.

BECOMING A LAWYER

—— 1859–1860 ——

Back in Erie, Strong needed to study for the bar exam. He also needed to find a lawyer who would act as his tutor and show him the procedures to follow in court.

The iron foundry's lawyer was a man named William S. Lane. He was one of the most respected lawyers in Erie, so BB went to his office to ask for his help.

"William, I was wondering if you could do me a favor?" BB asked.

"Sure, BB Just name it," Lane answered.

"My son Strong is home from college with a law degree. He needs someone to help him prepare for the bar exam."

"BB, I've known your boy for a long time. When I heard that he had graduated from Harvard with an interest in law, I was going to come and offer you my services. Bring him by, and I will show him around the office."

Strong was eager to get to work, and he showed up at Lane's office the following Monday. Lane worked on the first floor of a large building. The upstairs had apartments that he rented out. Each of the rooms in the law office was large and had expensive office furniture.

Lane met with Strong. "I'm happy to have you with me," he said. "Studying for the bar takes time. Don't think that you'll be ready to take it in 1859. Maybe you'll be ready sometime in 1860. It takes over four hundred hours of study before you're ready for the exam."

"I know that I have a lot of work to do, Mr. Lane, and I'm glad you're willing to help me out," Strong said as he followed Lane on a tour of the building.

"This is your office. You see all of those books on your desk? You need to read and learn from each one of them. You'll also clerk for me and do research on my ongoing cases. When I go to court, you go to court. You can't learn trial procedure sitting in your office. Do you have any questions?"

"Yes. Will I stay here after I become a lawyer, or do I practice law somewhere else?"

"Once you pass the bar, you'll be my partner. That's why I want you with me in the courtroom. You need to learn trial lawyering the right way."

In the 1800s, accused men often could not pay the high prices for a good lawyer. William Lane had high-profile clients, but he also took cases involving Erie residents who were less fortunate. Thanks largely to his smart real estate investments, Lane was one of the richest people in Erie. At that time, a lawyer earned more money in real estate than in the courtroom.

Strong soon saw why William Lane was such a respected lawyer. He was outstanding in the courtroom. He was an expert in questioning witnesses, he had a charm that members of the jury liked, and his final arguments were short and right to the point. To help Lane win his cases, Strong pored through law books looking for information.

But Strong went beyond studying law books. He started taking positions at City Hall, helping the Erie community, and he contributed to certain political races. It wasn't long before many people in Erie saw him as a very influential citizen.

Throughout it all, Strong continued to write letters to Elizabeth, still back in Connecticut. He wrote of marriage after he had finished taking the bar exam, and of raising a family and maintaining a religious life. But he also wrote about the looming uncertainty in their world, as the slavery question was getting more and more fraught with anxiety. He was unsure of how their life together would be altered if the South left the Union and civil war was declared. Elizabeth answered every letter, and she, too, was nervous about their future.

The country was locked in a gigantic philosophical battle. The South used slaves as an integral part of their economy; they were unwilling to free them and ruin the large cotton plantations. Most of the Northern states had banned slavery a long time ago and wanted the southern states to follow its lead. What held the country together was the fact that there were an equal number of slave states and slavery-free states. But as Americans moved west into new territories, a strain was put on that balance. Whispers of the South leaving the Union began to grow louder.

Ever since reading *Uncle Tom's Cabin* back at Trinity, Strong had held a firm belief that slavery was wrong. He and William Lane had many conversations on the subject, as Lane was like Strong—against slavery but not an abolitionist.

"You know that William Himrod, your dad's partner, is a big abolitionist," Lane said over coffee one morning.

"Yeah, he started that school for ex-slaves' children in his house. Do you think he hides slaves also?"

"I haven't heard that, but I wouldn't be surprised. It's hard to know how far you can go coming out against slavery nowadays, especially since the passage of the Fugitive Slave Law."

According to the law passed in 1852, Southern slave catchers were allowed to go into Northern states in the pursuit of runaway slaves. After its passage, the only way a runaway slave could truly be free was to make it to Canada.

Lane saw a copy of The True American on Strong's desk. In it, Henry Catlin, the publisher, wrote articles championing the abolition movement. The paper was printed in a building owned by state senator Morrow Barr Lowry, who was also an abolitionist.

"I see that you have a copy of Henry Catlin's newspaper. He likes to stir up trouble. You weren't here last April when Catlin brought Frederick Douglass to speak in Erie. There were a lot of people upset by Douglass' speech, and he and Catlin had to make a quick escape before violence broke out."

"I heard about it, but I don't know how far I should go getting involved in the antislavery issue."

"Well, Catlin also hides runaways in his paper bins over on Fifth and French. I think he's involved in the Underground Railroad."

The Underground Railroad was a series of shelters that helped runaway slaves escape to the North. Once they got to Erie, slaves would be hidden and then would sneak across Lake Erie to Canada on a boat in the middle of the night.

"I didn't know that. I just like reading his paper every week to see what he has to say. It only costs three cents."

"Don't leave that newspaper out where others may see it. Until this thing gets settled, it's hard to know who you can trust," Lane warned.

"I heard rumors that the Wesleyville Methodist Church is a stop on the Underground Railroad," Strong said, "but nobody knows for sure. Either way, I support the church by making donations."

"Be careful, Strong. Let's get to work on the Smiths' burglary case. We'll talk about slavery again some other time."

Trying to make sense of the world around him grew difficult for Strong. When he expressed this in his letters to Elizabeth, she worried about what would happen if war eventually broke out.

In October 1859, while Strong Vincent was studying for the bar exam, an abolitionist named John Brown and a band of his followers raided an arsenal at Harper's Ferry, Virginia. Brown had hoped that slaves in the area would leave their masters and join him in the insurrection. None of the slaves ran away. Then, a few days later, US Marines led by Robert E. Lee attacked Brown's group and ended the raid. Many articles about the raid appeared in the Erie newspaper. When Brown went on trial for treason, Senator Lowry helped him out with money for his defense.

Strong felt that things were moving toward a boiling point of discord between the two sides of the country, and he was going to have to decide soon what to do if war was declared.

Then, in early 1860, the new political party, the Republicans, nominated Abraham Lincoln for president. Lincoln promised to leave slave states alone, but to stop slavery's spread into the new territories. From the very first word he read about Lincoln, Strong was a believer. He helped organize events to support Lincoln, even though rumors persisted that if Lincoln was elected, the Southern states would secede.

In late 1860, three major events happened in Strong Vincent's life. The first was that he passed the bar exam and was sworn in as a lawyer. The second was that Abraham Lincoln was elected president. The third was that the Southern states did more than talk about secession; after Lincoln's election, they left the United States to form the Confederate States of America. South Carolina was the first to secede in December 1860.

By the time Lincoln gave his inaugural address in March 1861, seven states had left the Union. Lincoln reiterated that he would not interfere with slavery in the Southern states. He also said that if there were to be civil war, the South would have to be the one to initiate it. But he also said that secession was illegal.

With each new edition of the local newspaper, the Erie Observer, Strong read about the chaos in his country. He wrote to Elizabeth about his worries. Could he enlist in the army if it meant being away from her for a long time? Should they get married right away? Strong had a difficult time deciding what to do.

Then, in the spring of 1861, the South made it necessary for Strong to make his decision quickly.

THE ERIE BRIGADE
— 1861 —

On the morning of April 12, Confederate forces fired on Fort Sumter, a Union structure located in the harbor off the coast of Charleston, South Carolina. Word of the attack spread like wildfire, and Strong went into action.

On April 14 he met with Captain John McLane to enlist in the Wayne Guards. McLane had formed this militia group in 1859 as turmoil between North and South was coming to a boil. The Wayne Guards were ready to be called into action at a moment's notice. Its leader, Captain McLane, had fought in the Mexican War back in the 1840s. When he came back to Erie after the war, he was given a spot in the Erie Police Department. His experience in battle made him the best choice to lead.

"I would love to have you in my troop, Strong," McLane said after Strong had made his request. "In fact, I think you would make a good officer. You have become quite an influential person in the community. I think my soldiers would naturally respect you. I'll bring you in at the rank of second lieutenant. Does Mr. Lane know you are signing up with me?"

"Yes sir. He understands my sense of patriotic duty to my country."

"Good. We'll see you tonight at our barracks."

After work, Strong went home to tell his father what he had done.

"Dad, I feel I must serve my country in this time of uncertainty, so I have enlisted in the Wayne Guards. I talked to Captain McLane today, and he said he would make me second lieutenant."

"What about your law practice? Did you discuss this matter with William Lane?" BB understood his son's decision to enlist in the Wayne Guards, but he was worried about his life in Erie. He wished that events in the country were different for him.

"The Wayne Guards is just a militia right now, meaning I can do my lawyering during the day and do my soldiering at night."

"What about Elizabeth? I thought you two were making plans to marry," BB said.

"She knows of my desire to help this country in case of war and supports my decision. As for our marriage, once a brigade is formed in the Erie area, I'm going to send Elizabeth a telegram asking her to marry me."

"I support your decision to enlist, Strong. I wish the two of you could've been able to settle down and raise a family right away. This is a terrible time for you two to want to start a life on your own."

News of Fort Sumter ignited a patriotic fever in the Erie community. Citizens began flying American flags, and great pride in the president and country shone throughout the newspaper's editorials and in the talk around town. Then, on April 15, Abraham Lincoln called for seventy-five thousand volunteers to serve a ninety-day enlistment, inspiring Captain McLane to go to Harrisburg to speak with Governor Andrew Curtin about establishing a brigade of recruits from the Erie area. Before he left, he met with Strong.

"Lieutenant Vincent, while I am gone, I want you to work with the Wayne Guards on marching drills. Until I come back, hold off on enrolling new members. I hope to be able to sign up many more soldiers once the governor approves my proposal," Captain McLane told Strong as they met at the railroad station.

"I'll do my best to keep everything the way it is now," Strong responded. "But it might be hard considering the emotions many have after Lincoln's call for troops."

"Do your best, and I'll be back in a couple of days."

When Captain McLane returned to Erie, he returned as a colonel—

Governor Curtin had promoted him. He was also charged with raising a brigade of about eight hundred soldiers. Colonel McLane sent out a call for recruits, and he was overwhelmed with the response. Over twelve hundred men showed up. In order to follow Governor Curtin's orders, Colonel McLane turned away four hundred.

One of the first persons to sign up for the new brigade was Strong Vincent, whom Colonel McLane made first lieutenant.

Strong telegraphed Elizabeth as soon as he could, proposing marriage. Of course, Elizabeth said yes, but she wanted to be married in Jersey City, New Jersey, so that her sister Sarah could attend. Strong took a train to New Jersey. He was excited to meet Sarah and her husband, Theron Doremus. Strong and Elizabeth were married on April 25, 1861, in the Reformed Dutch Church. It was a big church in the middle of town. The four celebrated the matrimony, and then Strong and Lizzie boarded the next train back to Erie. When they arrived, an exciting homecoming awaited. BB gave them a big party to welcome the new addition to the family.

While Strong was getting married, Colonel McLane began building his group of enlisted soldiers. Since most of his recruits came from the Erie area, he named them the Erie Brigade. Needing a place for the soldiers to stay, he decided to use the Erie County Fairgrounds located on Buffalo Road. The soldiers named it "Camp McLane" after their leader. Immediately, local farmers began showing up with food, and Erie women got together to make uniforms—they did not want their boys going off to fight without looking presentable.

As soon as Strong rejoined them, the brigade was informed that they were to go to Pittsburgh, where they would meet other Pennsylvania troops. As they were getting ready to leave, the women arrived with more than seven hundred uniforms consisting of blue pants, yellow flannel shirts, and blue jackets. Colonel McLane organized a parade so that the soldiers could march through town as they headed to the railroad depot.

"I'm really going to miss you, Strong," Lizzie said.

"Well, you won't have to miss me much. I asked Colonel McLane if you could come with me down to Pittsburgh, and he said yes. You can stay at one of the hotels in town and help out where you can."

"I'm excited we can be together, even if it is for a short period each day. It would be hard to get married and have no contact with you right after."

On April 27, the Erie Brigade marched through Erie, and a large number of citizens showed up to cheer on their boys while Mehl's Brass Band played. The recruits looked smart in their new uniforms.

When they got to Pittsburgh, the brigade breakfasted in one of Pittsburgh's finest hotels, then marched through the city to more cheers. McLane's men were the first soldiers Pittsburghers had seen since Lincoln's call for service.

The soldiers marched outside the city to Camp Wilkins, which was located in the fairgrounds of Allegheny County and Western Pennsylvania. Colonel Phaon Jarrett, Camp Wilkins's director, had arranged for the soldiers to stay in large barns. Soldiers slept four soldiers to a cow stall, using straw for bedding and their knapsacks for pillows. Officers had a little better accommodation, and Strong prepared himself for his duties as lieutenant. He familiarized himself with the daily schedule. Reveille was announced at five thirty a.m. Breakfast was at seven, and Strong would begin drilling starting at nine. From then until six p.m., he made sure the soldiers drilled and drilled, only taking time out for lunch. Strong was in charge of running most of the marching exercises.

When the soldiers lined up for the first time, Lieutenant Vincent barked out the drilling orders. "About face! Right face! Forward march!" he yelled. When the recruits couldn't perform the march correctly, Strong yelled to help them get in a straight line. Then he yelled for the soldiers to halt and turn to face Colonel McLane. As the men halted, Strong heard a couple of the recruits laugh and make jokes about him.

"Make the guy an officer, and he thinks he's George Washington," one soldier said.

"Better do it right, or he'll scream at you," another laughed.

Upset, Strong was going to say something until he remembered what his father once said: "When things are bad, that's when you have to remain the calmest." He decided he would continue to bark out orders, both to let the soldiers know he was in charge and to show he was interested in molding them into well-trained soldiers.

Gradually, jokes about his conduct ceased. With no previous training as a soldier, Strong Vincent was quickly becoming a good military leader.

Elizabeth came to the camp every day and helped cook and serve the meals. She also helped the camp's doctor bandage the wounds of any soldier who got hurt. Soldiers began looking forward to seeing Elizabeth's smiling face each day.

When a soldier twisted an ankle during marching drills, it was Elizabeth who cared for him. She wrapped the ankle with a bandage.

"There. I hope I didn't tie it too tight!" she said.

"No, you did a fine job, and it sure is nice seeing a friendly face after staring at a bunch of hardened men all day. Thanks for being here for us every day."

"I'm just happy to be here near my husband and able to help out in some way."

After a few weeks, Camp Wilkins had grown to over eight thousand recruits. The Erie Brigade quickly distinguished themselves as one of the best units in marching. But there was a problem that was brought to Strong's attention.

"Lieutenant, it seems pretty stupid to march without rifles," one of the soldiers complained to Strong. "It's hard to act like real soldiers when you are marching with a tree limb or a mop handle."

"I'll ask Colonel McLane to put more pressure on the governor to get us outfitted with guns. We also need to have target practice, but we can't do that until we have rifles."

With McLane's insistence, rifles finally arrived at camp, and he took over training the soldiers. McLane bellowed orders louder than Vincent did and demanded even harsher discipline.

Every now and then, Strong and Lizzie were able to ride off together to spend a little bit of time alone in the countryside.

"I'm sorry we don't get to spend a lot of time together," Strong said after they had found a quiet place to talk.

"I'll take whatever time I can. It really isn't so bad. Your soldiers like me, and I get to see you every day, even if it is to just wave hello. I wish this thing between the North and South would hurry up and get over so that we can live our lives together."

"I wish for the same thing. The only problem is we are here in Pittsburgh. Some of the soldiers keep grumbling that we should be training in Washington."

Strong went to Colonel McLane with the men's complaints, and McLane sent a telegram to the Secretary of War wondering when he could bring his troops to Washington. He was told that there were too many recruits in the capital and thus he should stay put until his men were needed for battle.

Weeks went by, and the Erie Brigade stayed in Camp Wilkins. Grumbling increased. Their enlistment was only for ninety days, and they had been in Pittsburgh over half of that time.

Then a new problem arose.

"Lieutenant Vincent," Private Wells complained, "we've been here a long time, and none of us have gotten any money. A bunch of the other soldiers elected me as spokesperson to find out if we are ever gonna get paid."

Strong answered, "I understand your concern, but me and Colonel McLane haven't been paid either. I'm sure money is going to come."

"What about our families back in Erie? Are they supposed to eat promises?"

"I'll take the matter up with Colonel McLane right away. We'll figure out what the holdup is."

"You better, or we're leavin' on the next train north."

The grumbling about pay became louder, and discipline in drilling began to fall apart. Strong went to Colonel McLane.

"Colonel, sir, the troops are complaining that they haven't been paid. I told them you and I haven't gotten paid either, but that didn't do any good. Morale is low, and their marching is terrible."

"Tomorrow, get them ready for a hike!" Colonel McLane yelled. "I'll give the soldiers something to complain about!"

In the morning, Strong assembled the troops. Faced with McLane's icy stare as he inspected them, the soldiers had the air of children who had been caught with their hands in the cookie jar. After the inspection, Colonel McLane led the soldiers on a hike. When they were away from Camp Wilkins, McLane began to address them.

"It seems many of you are complaining about not getting paid yet. Well, Lieutenant Vincent and I haven't been paid either. Do you hear us crying about money? I love this country. I enlisted because I didn't think states had the right to break away from it and try to form their own country. We are all Americans, and I believe in my duty so much that I don't care if I ever get paid. I will soldier for no pay. If you want to complain, go home! If you want to stay here and restore this great country, join me in this mission. But there will be no more grumbling about pay. Is that understood?"

There was no more complaining, and no one left to go back to Erie. But soon the ninety-day enlistment would end.

Colonel McLane went to Washington himself to talk to Simon Cameron, the Secretary of War. With so many troops still in Washington, Cameron suggested that McLane's troops go back home. When Colonel McLane returned to Pittsburgh to tell his soldiers the disheartening news, he did make sure the troops received two months' pay.

Strong and Elizabeth took one last ride together through the Pittsburgh countryside.

"I'm disappointed we have to go back home," Strong said. "I was hoping to represent my country when we defeated the Confederates."

"I know, Strong, but I have watched you grow into an impressive leader. Your soldiers have really come to respect you. You didn't waste your time down here."

"One good thing about going back to Erie is that we can be together full-time."

"It'll be nice to spend time with you and your family."

Back in Erie, a huge crowd had gathered to welcome back their men. It did not matter that they never saw action. To the townsfolk, the soldiers of the Erie Regiment were all heroes.

When they got back to Erie, Strong and Lizzie lived at Strong's father's house because neither knew if Strong would one day go back into the army.

"So, how did you like being in the army?" BB asked his son when they got home.

"I really liked it. I felt comfortable leading the troops in drill. After a while, I think they really responded to my leadership."

"They liked Strong a lot," Lizzy added. "I would talk with the soldiers in the kitchen, and some of them told me Strong was a good leader."

"If Lincoln asks for more recruits, do you think you would enlist again?" BB wanted to know.

"I'll be the first in line. I'm committed to serving my country and to bringing the South back into the Union. If Lincoln needs me again, I wouldn't hesitate."

Strong introduced his wife to William Lane, and she helped clean around the law office. The two were able to act like a married couple for the first time. They both cherished the time together. They would ride out of town on horses and bring a picnic lunch to share. But always, the shadow of war loomed over their future.

In the early part of the war, both the North and the South thought it would be a short conflict, decided by one big battle. If the North won, the South would come running back to the United States. If the South won, the North would give up trying to make the South come back.

The problem was that the result of the first big battle was not either of those two outcomes, and it would signal the end of the time Lizzie and Strong could spend together.

THE 83RD PENNSYLVANIA
— 1861 —

The big battle everyone was waiting for finally occurred on July 21 near Manassas, Virginia, along Bull Run Creek. The Union Army experienced an early advantage, but soon the South, strengthened by reinforcements, beat back the North, causing Union soldiers to flee the thirty miles back to Washington, DC. For the president, it was a sobering lesson: the war was going to take a long time to win. The next day, on July 22, Lincoln called for five hundred thousand volunteers to serve three years of service.

Governor Curtin charged Colonel McLane with building a unit of one thousand recruits. Strong enlisted right away, but only a little more than three hundred of the soldiers who served in the Erie Brigade joined him. It would take them more than a month to reach the required number of recruits. McLane brought the new soldiers back to the Erie County Fairgrounds. Farmers once again helped out with food, but there wasn't the constant marching. The soldiers wanted to make sure they were going to Washington before giving up their days to drilling.

When McLane finally had more than one thousand recruits, he sent a telegram to the governor. Curtin sent Captain Bell of the United States Army to Erie to swear in the soldiers. They would not be called the Erie Brigade anymore; as part of the US Army, they were the 83rd Pennsylvania Regiment of Volunteers.

Colonel McLane wanted the soldiers to vote for their officers. McLane was unanimously voted as the regiment's leader, at the rank of colonel. Second-in-command was Strong Vincent at the rank of major. Even though Strong had no military training, his leadership in the Erie Brigade at Fort Wilkins showed he had strong leadership skills.

On September 9, Colonel McLane met with Strong.

"Captain Bell assured me that we are going to Washington. I am going to stay behind to organize things here, but being second-in-command, I want you to go on ahead so when we get off the train in Washington, we have a camp with supplies. The soldiers will need uniforms, guns, ammunition, tents, and food."

"Don't worry, Colonel," Strong said. "I'll have everything ready when you arrive."

Strong got ready to board a train to Washington. This time, Elizabeth would be staying behind. The Vincent family gathered at the depot to see him off.

"Goodbye, Lizzie," Strong said. "Never forget that I love you. Remember my mission. I believe that we will win this war and reunite the country. I hope to return, but if I am killed in battle, remember that I gave my life for an honorable cause."

"I love you, Strong. Remember, you'll always be my hero. I'll write to you as often as I can. Take care of yourself," Lizzie responded as the two shared one last embrace.

As soon as Strong arrived in Washington, he worked hard to acquire everything Colonel McLane had requested. He secured land for their camp at Hall's Hill, Virginia. About twenty miles west of Washington, DC, it was also twenty miles away from where troops had fought on the Bull Run battlefield. Southern soldiers still remained in the area.

It took a few days for the train carrying the 83rd Pennsylvania to reach Washington. It pulled into the train depot on September 19. When the regiment arrived at their camp, one of its first duties was to stand guard to make sure the Confederates did not attack. Each night saw shooting back and forth between the Confederate and Union troops, but no one was ever injured.

The 83rd was a part of General Fitz John Porter's Fifth Corps, which was divided into two divisions. The 83rd was a part of General George Morell's First Division. Each division was broken into brigades. The 83rd was in the Third Brigade, which was led by General Dan Butterfield. Along with the 83rd Pennsylvania, the Third Brigade was composed of the 17th New York, the 44th New York, and the 16th Michigan regiments. All four regiments were camped on Hall's Hill.

Eager for the men to get to know the other regiments in the Third Brigade, Colonel McLane sent Strong to ask their neighbors, the 44th New York, to dine with them one evening. Colonel Stephen Stryker, the head of the New York regiment, was happy to accept, beginning what would become an important relationship. Throughout the war, the two regiments always fought side by side, earning the nickname "Butterfield's Twins" since the general always placed them next to each other in battle. As the war continued, both regiments counted on each other in case of trouble.

As the 83rd got settled, drilling started up again in earnest. General Butterfield was a strict disciplinarian when it came to the exactness of drill, bellowing even louder than Colonel McLane or Major Vincent. Butterfield had the soldiers of the Third Brigade move forward together, move to the right or left as one, and carry their rifles in a specific way. The brigade underwent hundreds of hours of practice to be sure that it would know what to do when the soldiers were in battle. And much like back at Camp Wilkins, it was Major Vincent who led the 83rd in marching most days.

Colonel McLane was in charge of target shooting and the practice of quickly reloading the soldiers' Springfield muskets, which could only fire one shot before they had to be reloaded. McLane wanted his soldiers to be able to load quickly enough that they could accurately fire two times in one minute.

At night, Strong studied books about how to fight a tactical battle. He was constantly reporting to General Butterfield, who quizzed him on the information. He must have done well, for in October, Strong was promoted to lieutenant colonel.

As the months wore on, soldiers were still drilling and standing guard for more than fourteen hours per day. Under General Butterfield's, Colonel McLane's, and Lieutenant Colonel Vincent's leadership, the 83rd became one of the most accomplished drill marching units the North had.

One day, as Strong was leading the regiment through a drill, the head of the Army of the Potomac, Major General George McClellan, appeared. When he saw the precision with which Strong was leading the soldiers, he called Colonel McLane over.

"Who is that leading your soldiers in drill?" General McClellan asked.

"That's my second-in-command, Lieutenant Colonel Strong Vincent, sir."

"Well, you tell that man he is doing a fine job. I do believe your regiment is one of the finest in the entire army. Very good, Colonel."

By November, the soldiers were getting impatient to fight, so General McClellan held a contest to see which regiment marched the best drills. Led by Strong's commands, the 83rd won. For a prize, the soldiers were fitted for a new kind of uniform modeled after that of the soldiers in the French Foreign Legion. It was called a Zouave uniform, and it consisted of a blue shirt and a short blue jacket with red trim, baggy red pants, and white gaiters that fit over the top of the shoe and extended up to just below the knee. The only problem was that when the new uniforms arrived, they were too small to fit thirty percent of the soldiers.

"Most of those uniforms are too small to use in battle," Colonel McLane told the soldiers. "We are not going to dress in them at all."

There was grumbling among the soldiers, who wanted to wear their new uniforms whether they fit or not. They complained to Strong, who approached Colonel McLane to try to persuade him to change his mind. To appease the soldiers, Colonel McLane came up with an alternative.

"If we are marching in a parade, you can wear the new uniforms, but when we go into battle, you will switch back to the Union blue uniform. That's the best I can do."

The soldiers were disappointed. There were only a few parades, and many of the uniforms were never worn at all.

The soldiers remained in Washington throughout the winter, with only their tents and campfires to keep them warm at night. Strong would cancel drilling if there was snow on the ground or the cold wind was too harsh.

One benefit of staying put was that it gave Strong an opportunity to bring Lizzie in for a visit. Lizzie went into the camp to see soldiers she had met back at Camp Wilkins. She and Strong were also able to dine in one of the nicest restaurants in Washington. Afterward, they strolled through the streets.

"Do you know when you and the soldiers will move out of Washington?" she asked Strong.

"I don't know. The soldiers are getting cranky sitting around in the cold. They want to get at the enemy. President Lincoln and his cabinet are also disappointed General McClellan is still here."

"At least staying in Washington gave us some time to be together. This is such a beautiful city," she said as she grabbed Strong's hand.

"It is, but I miss Erie," Strong said as they continued their walk through the tree-lined streets.

By March, the Union Army had been in Washington for six months without any action. Not only were the soldiers complaining, but President Lincoln was pressuring General McClellan to do something.

Finally, on March 9, General Butterfield called Colonel McLane to his headquarters.

"Colonel McLane, I want the regiment ready to march first thing in the morning. Tell the soldiers they will need three days of rations."

"That's good news, General. The men have been itching to get out of here and get into some real fighting."

When Colonel McLane told the 83rd the news, the soldiers eagerly packed their belongings under the watchful eyes of Lieutenant Colonel Vincent and Colonel McLane, who wanted to make sure their unit was ready for battle.

Reveille sounded early in the morning of March 10. The soldiers rushed to make a small breakfast, then got into marching formation. Their orders were to join the almost one hundred thousand soldiers who would be taking part in McClellan's assault on any Confederate units still in the area.

The soldiers took two different roads to speed up their march. Spirits were high, and the cool weather of springtime meant that the marching wasn't strenuous, although each man was lugging over forty pounds of food and gear. By nightfall, the soldiers of the 83rd were setting up camp by the Fairfax Courthouse. It had been a twelve-mile march, and Strong and Colonel McLane walked through the camp congratulating the soldiers on their first real hike.

"Get some sleep," McLane told them. "Reveille will be early again tomorrow. We'll hit Centerville by noon. Then we'll show the Rebs what the Eighty-Third Pennsylvania is made of."

The soldiers let out a great cheer.

In the morning, however, there was no early reveille. Colonel McLane came to address his men.

"It seems that when word got out that such a large force was coming at them; all the Confederates in Centerville and Manassas ran away to Gordonsville, some ninety miles away. Look at that! Our first victory came without firing a single shot!"

The soldiers of the 83rd let out another great cheer.

As the soldiers of all four regiments of the Third Brigade gathered to march again, General McClellan rode by on his horse. Cheers greeted him; all admired the great general who won battles without any casualties.

The entire day was one big party. Regimental bands played music, and by nightfall the soldiers were exhausted from celebrating.

While some of McClellan's force marched back to Washington, General Butterfield was told to keep his brigade in the area. Strong and Colonel McLane had the soldiers march the seven miles to Centerville to observe the forts constructed by the Southern soldiers. Then they went a few more miles to the Manassas battlefield, where they saw the structures Rebel soldiers had dug into the surrounding hills in order to shelter from the elements. Members of the 83rd were envious; they froze in their tents all winter, but these structures looked like they had kept the Rebel soldiers warm. Strong told them to stop whining and study how the structures were made so that maybe they could make similar ones in the future.

On March 15, the 83rd Pennsylvania began its march back toward Washington. During the trip, the regiment's destination was changed to Alexandria, Virginia. The soldiers marched in a cold rain that dampened their spirits. It was the first time the regiment had to march in the rain, but it would not be the last. There would be many more wet marches throughout the war.

THE PENINSULA CAMPAIGN: YORKTOWN

— 1862 —

When the soldiers of the 83rd Regiment reached Alexandria, Virginia, they were tired and wet from the long march in the rain.

Colonel McLane gathered the soldiers and told them General McClellan's plan to win the war. The unit was to board a steamer that would take them down the Potomac River to the Chesapeake Bay. Then they would switch to another boat that would take them to Hampton, Virginia, on the edge of the James River. McClellan's plan was to go up the James River to eventually reach the Confederate capital of Richmond and end the war. After all, McClellan's forces vastly outnumbered the Confederates.

The 83rd, along with the 44th New York, 16th Michigan, and 17th New York, boarded the first boat on the morning of March 22, and on March 24, they arrived at Hampton and built a camp for the night.

For a week, they endured huge rainstorms that made the area look like a swamp and kept them from lighting campfires. When the unit received their next marching orders, the soldiers were happy to leave the camp behind.

The Third Brigade, still being led by General Butterfield, was ordered to invade and capture an area known as Big Bethel, where the Confederates had constructed a large earthworks in 1861 that guarded a church and a courthouse sitting at the crossroads. The 83rd was chosen to have the honor of planting their battle flag at the courthouse if the invasion was successful. The color bearer usually carried the regimental flag, but now the soldiers argued over who should be the one to plant it.

The night before the invasion, a few veteran soldiers who had attempted to capture the same fortress in late 1861 came over to talk to members of the 83rd.

"I hear you're goin' after Big Bethel in the mornin'," one soldier said. "Well, last year we tried to take it, but when we made our charge, the Rebs pounded us with cannons. We took a whole bunch of casualties before retreating. General John Magruder's still there with all his cannons. You better take care tomorrow, or he'll blow you apart like he did us."

More than one member of the 83rd got a little nervous after hearing the story. Strong and Colonel McLane spent the rest of the night inspiring the troops and getting them ready for battle by complimenting them on their readiness.

Early in the morning on March 27, 1862, General Butterfield led his brigade up the road leading to Big Bethel. It was hot and humid, making the march difficult.

When they arrived at the battle site around noon, the terrain was not encouraging. Directly in front of them was a thick area of woods, and beyond that, two to three hundred yards of wide-open ground separated them from the ten-foot-high mound the Confederates had constructed. The Rebels would be firing at them from its top, and the concealed cannon would also be blasting away. They were going to have to run as fast as they could over the open ground and then climb the hill with bullets and cannonballs flying. As the soldiers looked over the area, a sense of nervousness grew.

General Butterfield aligned his four regiments. On the far right were the 16th Michigan and the 17th New York. On the far left were the 83rd Pennsylvania and the 44th New York.

"Remember all the training we've gone through," Strong told his soldiers, seeing their edginess. "As you run across the open field, don't fire your rifle. If you do, you're going to have to stop and reload it in a vulnerable position. Just keep running. Save the ammunition until you get to the earthworks." At that point he cried out, "Bayonets!" and the soldiers complied by attaching their bayonets to their rifles.

Colonel McLane approached. "We all enlisted in the army for this moment. It's time to show these Rebels what the Eighty-Third is made of. Show the enemy no mercy!"

General Butterfield ordered the unit forward. The woods were filled with briars and swampy areas, and the soldiers struggled through it. The briars were tearing up their skin.

Once they reached the edge of the woods, Colonel McLane called for the soldiers to yell as loud as they could as they made their run across the field.

The soldiers were eager to attack the Confederate force. When Colonel McLane shouted, "Charge!" the soldiers all let out a loud whoop and began running.

Once they had gone twenty yards, the soldiers began wondering why they hadn't been fired upon. Were the Confederates waiting for them to hit the earthworks before opening fire? Remembering Lieutenant Colonel Vincent's order not to fire at the enemy, they ran faster.

Then they hit the earthworks, where they began scaling the muddy hill. Once they reached the summit, they found no enemy soldiers on the other side. General Magruder had pulled his soldiers out days before. A few lingering Confederate cavalrymen fired a few harmless shots and raced away once they saw the Union soldiers.

Like before at Centerville and Manassas, they had come to a battlefield only to find no enemy to fight.

There was also no church or courthouse for the 83rd to plant their flag in front of, so James McKinley, the color sergeant, planted the battle flag at the top of Big Bethel's earthworks. As he did so, the soldiers let out a roar of victory. There were no casualties—the only wounds from the charge were caused by the briars in the woods.

The soldiers camped at Big Bethel for several days. It was Strong's job to take some soldiers and scope out the area, looking for enemy soldiers. When they didn't find any, the Third Brigade headed back to their camp.

In early April, General McClellan wasted no time moving his sixty-seven thousand soldiers toward Yorktown, some twenty-five miles away.

The first day of their forward movement was an easy march, but on the second day, it rained, turning the road into a muddy mess and trapping the wagons carrying weapons and ammunition in a knee-deep quagmire. If a soldier's boots weren't tied tight, he lost them in the mud.

Strong did his best to keep the soldiers moving, but they quickly developed a sour mood. The six miles they marched that day were the hardest miles the 83rd would march throughout the war. It took a couple of more days to finally reach the outskirts of Yorktown.

Yorktown was a small village with thick walls surrounding it, presenting a unique challenge. In some places, the walls were thirty feet high, and cannons guarded the entry to the fort, as did a wide-open plain that made invasion a deadly prospect.

Confederate General Magruder, who had fled the earthworks at Big Bethel, was defending the fort against McClellan's men. Magruder had only fifteen thousand men against four times that many Union soldiers, as the other parts of the Confederate Army were scattered across Virginia. The Confederate leader, General Joseph Johnston, told Magruder to keep McClellan in Yorktown until Johnston could bring his forces together.

To do this, Magruder knew he had to make McClellan think he had more soldiers than he possessed, so he constantly paraded his men in front of McClellan from behind Yorktown's walls. He also painted big trees black to make them look like cannons. The scheme worked, as McClellan became convinced that he was facing more than one hundred thousand soldiers with heavy artillery.

Hesitant to lose soldiers in a direct attack, McClellan decided to lay siege to the town. A siege is a long engagement where the attacking army blocks the defenders in their fort and keeps supplies from entering. Meanwhile, the attacking army digs trenches as close as possible to the defenses and uses big, long-range cannons to blast holes in the enemy fort. After a length of time, the soldiers attack, racing from the trenches to run through the holes the big guns created.

The Fifth Corps, led by General Porter, occupied the extreme right of the Union forces. Porter was impressed by how Strong conducted himself and arranged a meeting as the 83rd set up camp behind a wooded area.

"Lieutenant Colonel, you are doing very well, especially seeing that you did not go to West Point for military training. I want you to be my aide during this siege. I'll run all of my orders through you, and I want you to study the different things that go into a siege. You'll report back to me every night with your information."

"Thank you, sir," Strong answered. Being General Porter's aide was quite an honor. "I'll do my best to not let you down."

"Your first assignment is to dig a long trench. When we finally attack, we'll use your trench to begin our assault. Every regiment under my command will be out there digging with you. The trench should start out at three feet wide and three feet deep. The soldiers will make it larger as the trench gets longer. You should hold your digging detail until after dark. That way you won't be dodging enemy bullets."

"We'll begin digging tonight, sir," Strong said.

Strong divided his soldiers into three groups for digging the trenches. When one group got tired, the next group would relieve them.

That first night, the Confederates did not see the soldiers digging, and so the groups worked safely. Eventually, however, the trenches were spotted. Although Rebel forces fired at them periodically, there were very few injuries.

Meanwhile, Strong studied the siege, reporting how many cannons were brought in and where they were located, how much ammunition was fired each day, how the big guns were aimed, and where the cannons were placed in order to fire on the enemy while still protecting the soldiers firing them. He learned new types of battle tactics, not through books, but through experience and observation. He wanted to be ready if he ever was in charge of another siege.

After a few days, the Confederates brought their cannon over so that they could fire at the soldiers' trench-digging crews. Seeing the men's nervousness, Strong decided he needed sentries to warn the diggers that a cannon blast was coming. He joined the soldiers and served as one of the lookouts.

When he saw the flash coming from inside the fort, Strong yelled, "Incoming! Take cover!"

The digging soldiers jumped at once to find refuge. With their lieutenant colonel's help, the 83rd continued to suffer only a few injuries.

In response, the Union soldiers brought up a couple of two-hundred-pound cannons called "Parrott rifles." When fired at night, the huge cannons lit up the night sky and shook the ground as if there were an earthquake.

Both sides blasted away at each other all night, every night. As the trenches got longer, the time for the attack approached.

On May 3, the trenches were almost finished. Soldiers had been digging for almost one month. Strong was in General Porter's headquarters with his daily report when all of a sudden, the Confederates unloaded a huge barrage of cannon fire, sending the soldiers scrambling to find safe places to survive the onslaught.

"General Porter, sir. You should take cover," a nervous Strong pleaded.

General Porter, however, was calm, as if nothing out of the ordinary was going on. "I'm okay. Hear all of that cannon fire? The Rebs are getting ready to run," he said.

"How do you know?" Strong asked.

"They're trying to use up their ammunition. That way when they retreat, they won't be leaving weaponry for us to take."

"Do you think General McClellan knows this?" Strong asked.

"He should. Go to General Butterfield and tell him to have the troops in the trenches at first light. It's time to attack. I'll alert the other regiments to be ready. Good luck tomorrow."

Strong reported to General Butterfield and Colonel McLane and gave them General Porter's order.

"Did you know the South was getting ready to retreat?" Strong asked Colonel McLane.

"I know a heavy artillery barrage means the enemy is up to something."

As Colonel McLane gathered the soldiers, he learned the army had already experienced a close call. The drummer boy was hiding in his tent when a cannonball tore through the structure and went right through his drum. Although it was cause for laughter, it was still a scary incident.

The 83rd marched into the trenches as the sun began to rise. Soldiers did not know what to expect; while they had heard rumors that the Confederates had pulled out, none were verified. General Porter appeared to inspect his forces.

"Lieutenant Colonel Vincent, you and your men did a fine job making these trenches."

After one last look up and down his line, General Porter gave the order to charge.

The soldiers jumped out of the trenches and ran toward the fort. Even though they were getting closer and closer to Yorktown, there was no enemy fire. General Magruder had indeed pulled his forces out of town. It was another battle where one side did not show up.

When General McClellan entered Yorktown later that day, cheers from the soldiers greeted him once again. It was another bloodless victory, and one that earned Strong Vincent respect from many of the Union's important generals.

However, Yorktown marked the end of easy victories for the 83rd. If they were going to win (or lose) battles in the future, they would have to pay for them in blood.

THE PENINSULA CAMPAIGN: HANOVER COURTHOUSE

—— 1862 ——

After the victory at Yorktown, General McClellan moved the Army of the Potomac up the York River by boat instead of marching.

General Butterfield's Third Brigade, with the 17th New York regiment added to the other four regiments, spent a couple of days floating up to West Point, Virginia—where the York River ended and split into two smaller rivers. The next evening, General Butterfield and Colonel McLane brought Strong in to tell him about a new mission.

"We received word of Confederate soldiers nearby," General Butterfield told him. "I don't know how many there are or where they are located, but reports indicate they are near Custis Pond."

"I want you to take two companies and find the enemy," Colonel McLane said. "We have a contraband named Jones who will help you with the terrain. I want you to find the Rebels and run them out of here. Take as many prisoners as you can. They may provide us with important information about the enemy."

"Yes, sir. I'll have the soldiers ready first thing in the morning," Strong answered, proud that these two senior officers trusted him to lead the mission all by himself.

In the morning, Strong and approximately three hundred soldiers left camp. Jones, a contraband ex-slave who had escaped from his master a few days earlier, helped lead them through the woods.

"Thisaway, suh," Jones said to the lieutenant colonel. "Y'all be careful. There's some nasty rattler snakes 'round here."

"Jones, I want to head toward the river in that direction," Strong said as he pointed.

"Yes, suh. It gonna get a little swampy dat way, but I'll show you how to sneak 'round the water."

The morning was humid, making marching difficult again. Strong and his group hiked more than ten miles before Jones stopped in front of a big hill.

"You goes over dat hill yonder and y'all will see the Custis Pond. Dat's where the Rebs are s'posed to be," Jones said.

"Thanks, Jones. You stay here so you can guide us back after we're done." Then Strong called to his soldiers. "All right, men. Be ready to charge once we get over the hill."

The unit climbed as fast as they could, and when they reached the top, the members of the 83rd got ready to charge down the other side toward the enemy. They let out a loud yell, but there were no Confederate soldiers on the other side.

"Are you sure there are Confederate soldiers anywhere? Maybe they're a figment of our imagination. Everywhere we go, we never see any," one of the soldiers joked. The other soldiers laughed.

"Don't worry," Strong said. "Before this war is over, you'll have seen your fill of Confederate soldiers. You'll be wishing for battles where there is no enemy." He surveyed the empty hill. "I want each company to go in a different direction and make sure the enemy is nowhere around here."

The soldiers found no evidence of any Confederate presence, and then they returned back to camp. Their record of avoiding face-to-face contact with the Rebels remained intact. Strong led the disappointed group back to West Point.

After a few more restful days, General McClellan told General Butterfield to march his brigade to the Chickahominy River, about forty-seven miles away.

It was pouring rain as the soldiers left, and Strong rode on horseback instead of marching through the sloppy terrain. The following day, the weather was humid and the temperature climbed into the eighties, an equally uncomfortable situation given the fact that Union uniforms were made of wool and soldiers carried backpacks weighing almost seventy pounds. Still, the Third Brigade made progress that day and every day until it reached its destination.

On May 23, the Third Corps finally made it to Cold Harbor, near the Chickahominy River. Progress up the Peninsula had been slow, but McClellan's army was more than three-quarters of the way to Richmond.

The soldiers camped at Cold Harbor for two days before Colonel McLane called the 83rd together and told the men to be ready to march at four a.m. the next morning. The soldiers were to attack Hanover Courthouse, where Confederate soldiers were supposed to be dug in.

It was raining again as the brigade began its march. By noon, the rain had subsided, and the heat and humidity took over. By three o'clock, McLane's brigade had marched eighteen miles and had begun to hear the sounds of heavy artillery.

As the Third Brigade took a break, General John Martindale of the First Brigade came to General Butterfield.

"I am getting pounded by artillery. Can you spare a regiment to help me out?"

"I'll give you the Forty-Fourth New York," Butterfield said. "It's one of my best."

The 44th went with General Martindale, and Butterfield moved the rest of the Third Brigade forward. The fighting to their right—where the 44th was heading—was getting heated.

Butterfield stopped his brigade in front of a thick area of woods, not wanting to walk into an ambush. Having no other way to spot the enemy, he climbed up a tree to see if there were Rebel soldiers on the other side of the woods.

"I see enemy soldiers ahead of us, but I can't make out how many," General Butterfield called down.

"Lieutenant Colonel Vincent!" Colonel McLane called out. "Form a skirmish party of Company A and Company B, and then go up through the woods and find out how many soldiers are in our front."

"Yes, sir," Strong said. "I'll send word back as fast as I can."

Strong led his group into the woods. As they came to a clearing, he spotted the Confederates and sent for one of the soldiers from Company A.

"Tell Colonel McLane we outnumber the enemy. He needs to bring up the Third Brigade as fast as he can."

The Confederates, who were beyond the woods, were from North Carolina, led by General Lane. These soldiers had fought at a different point on the battlefield, and they had retreated to the spot in front of the Third Brigade. When Lane saw the Yankee soldiers charging from the woods, he had no choice but to retreat again, leaving his only piece of artillery, a large cannon, behind for the 17th New York to capture. As the Rebels were running, the 83rd also captured three or four prisoners.

General Butterfield interrogated the captured soldiers and found out that more Confederates were advancing behind them. Leaving the 12th and 17th New York regiments to hold the area, Butterfield took the 16th Michigan and the 83rd Pennsylvania back toward this new threat.

"We have to move fast," he said. "Instead of working our way through the woods, use the area by the railroad tracks. The land is clear that way."

The soldiers did as he ordered and ran toward the enemy—only they had already marched almost thirty miles in the heat that day, and some keeled over due to dehydration.

The soldiers came to a small cluster of trees about three hundred yards from the enemy.

Turning to his soldiers, Colonel McLane shouted, "This is why we joined the army! When we burst through the trees, let these Rebels know how tough Pennsylvanians are!"

Cheers went up and down the line.

But as soon as the soldiers stepped out of the woods, they were staring down the barrels of hundreds of Confederate rifles.

"Get down!" Colonel McLane yelled just before the first volley.

The soldiers immediately went down to the ground, and what seemed like a wall of bullets passed harmlessly overhead.

Then McLane yelled, "Get up and fire!"

As the gray-clad soldiers were reloading, the 83rd Pennsylvania and the 16th Michigan unleashed their own wall of bullets. Many of the enemy soldiers went down.

McLane yelled, "Fire at will. Give it to them!"

The two armies stood toe-to-toe, firing into each other. After a few more rounds, General Branch of the 28th North Carolina regiment ordered his soldiers to retreat. The 83rd Pennsylvania and the 16th Michigan chased after the enemy and took some more prisoners, but the fighting was over for the day. It was getting dark, and to press forward would expose the soldiers to needless risk.

The 83rd rejoiced that they had made the enemy retreat two times that day. What was more, the regiment only had eight injured soldiers and no deaths (although a couple of days later, one of the injured soldiers died from his wounds). The regiment also captured one hundred and eighteen Confederate soldiers.

The 44th New York had faced heavier fire after joining the First Brigade. They lost twenty-five soldiers, and another sixty were injured.

General McClellan rode among the soldiers, praising them on the victory. The Union Army was now twelve miles from the Rebel capital, and it looked like his army would have an easy time defeating the Confederate Army, thanks in part to the Third Brigade. McClellan wanted to reward General Butterfield for his efforts on the battlefield with a pair of golden spurs. He ordered Colonel McLane to have a ceremony to present them on short notice.

Colonel McLane decided to give the assignment to Strong. He was able to get a certificate made in the town of Hanover before gathering the soldiers of the Third Brigade. General McClellan also attended the ceremony.

"General Butterfield," Strong announced. "General McClelland and other officers of the Third Corps would like to honor you for your leadership at the Battle of Hanover Courthouse on May 27, 1862. They would also like give you these golden spurs as a token of their admiration."

He handed them to Butterfield along with the certificate, and the soldiers cheered loudly for their leader. The small ceremony lasted only a few minutes, but it helped Strong Vincent rise in the esteem of not only General Butterfield, but also General McClellan.

The good feelings created by the victory at Hanover Courthouse would be one of the brightest moments for McClellan in the Peninsula Campaign. After that, cheering assemblies would be hard to come by.

THE PENINSULA CAMPAIGN: GAINES' MILL

—— 1862 ——

After the victory at Hanover Courthouse, General McClellan took his time moving his army forward.

For a few weeks, life was easy for Strong. The day began at four thirty a.m. Then, from five thirty to six thirty, Strong was in charge of putting the soldiers through drills. The rest of the day was spent hanging around camp, until a five-p.m. drill officially ended the day.

On May 31, the Union Army fought the Confederates at Seven Pines. While the 83rd could hear the gunfire, they did not take part in the battle, in which the Confederate leader General Joseph Johnston was wounded. His replacement was General Robert E. Lee, who would prove to be much more aggressive than Johnston. General McClellan was about to face a new kind of foe on the battlefield.

Meanwhile, as the soldiers continued to camp around the Chickahominy River, they were already facing a new kind of foe, one that did not come bearing a rifle. From the swamps that lined the river's bank emerged a disease called the Chickahominy Fever, a combination of malaria and typhoid. After doctors treated several cases, they determined that the disease was spread by the many mosquitoes that inhabited the area.

The first sign of the illness was an elevated temperature, followed by vomiting and diarrhea. As a sick soldier's body temperature climbed, he developed chills and pains. The longer the illness, the more the patient was at risk for liver and kidney failure. Once a soldier became unconscious, death was a worry.

Not everyone who came down with Chickahominy Fever faced all of the symptoms. There were many light cases. But for the soldiers camping near the Chickahominy, a mosquito bite always bred a fear that sickness might follow.

One of the first members of the 83rd to come down with Chickahominy Fever was Colonel McLane, although he had a minor case and recovered rapidly. Others in the regiment weren't so lucky. More than one hundred and thirty 83rd Pennsylvania soldiers were hospitalized with Chickahominy Fever. Of those infected, twenty-six died.

Toward the end of June, the 83rd moved camp to prepare for the next battle. It had been almost a month since they had fought at Hanover Courthouse, and the next battle would be at Gaines' Mill. Colonel McLane ordered the soldiers forward. But there was something wrong with Strong. He was having a hard time riding in the saddle. He was afraid that the disease that had taken down so many soldiers had now affected him. When the soldiers camped for the night, General Butterfield and Colonel McLane came to visit.

"Lieutenant Colonel Vincent, I think that you may have the disease that's been goin' 'round the camp. I suggest you check into the field hospital right away," Butterfield said.

"I'll be fine by the morning, General. If not, then I'll see the doctor tomorrow," Strong answered.

"No, it's best you treat this thing right away," Colonel McLane objected. "I went to be seen by the doctors as soon as possible, and I got better in a hurry."

"But we may go into battle tomorrow. The men need me," Strong said.

"If we go into battle tomorrow, then we need as many healthy soldiers as we can muster, not sick ones. I am ordering you to report to the field hospital," General Butterfield said, which ended the discussion.

Strong went to the big white tent that served as a field hospital. As soon as the doctors set eyes on him, he was helped to a bed. His temperature was over one hundred degrees. He began to get sick to his stomach. Going to the hospital was clearly the right thing to do, yet Strong yearned to be with his soldiers on the eve of a big battle.

In the morning, General Butterfield led the Third Brigade out of camp and found a good defensive position, lining the 83rd up next to the 44th New York. Behind them, Butterfield placed the 16th Michigan and the 12th New York.

Colonel McLane surveyed the battlefield. Directly in front of the Third Brigade's position was a swampy area. Beyond the swamp was a clearing of about three hundred yards, and behind that a wooded area. The Confederates would have to cross the open field and the swamp to reach McLane's position. To make their position even stronger, he ordered the soldiers to chop down trees to fortify their defensive position and to cover themselves as they fired.

To the right of the Third Brigade was the First Brigade, led by General Martindale. Their defensive position was good, but it was not as fortified.

Right before the battle started, Colonel McLane received a message from General Butterfield that said he was to hold his position at all costs.

"That was a waste of the general's time," he told the messenger. "You tell the general I have no intention of giving up this position."

The soldiers could hear the Rebels making their way through the woods. When they appeared in the open, Colonel McLane yelled for his soldiers to let them have it. All up and down the line, the soldiers of the 44th and 83rd fired into the enemy. Scores of enemy soldiers went down under the attack. Finally, they retreated into the woods.

Although the enemy force made three more charges from the woods, they were beaten back by the First and Third Brigades every time. Colonel McLane shouted encouragement after each charge was repulsed.

Unfortunately for Butterfield's sturdy brigades, at that point,

Confederate General James Longstreet showed up with a fresh corps of reinforcements. The next time the Rebels emerged from the woods, the soldiers of the 83rd couldn't believe the size of the new attacking force. The Pennsylvanians had no way of knowing this, but Longstreet's charge at Gaines' Mill was one of the largest infantry charges of the entire war.

Seeing that the First Brigade's position would be easier to take than the Third's, General Longstreet ordered his soldiers to concentrate on General Martindale's men. The First Brigade stood its ground for as long as it could, but their soldiers finally began to run in retreat, leaving the Third Brigade alone as it faced the huge wave of attackers. Colonel McLane kept the 44th in position, but he moved the 83rd so that it formed a right angle to the New Yorkers and better prevented the Rebels from surrounding them.

As the enemy came on, Colonel McLane was shot once in the upper body and once in the head. Soldiers ran to him, but he had died before hitting the ground. That left Major Louis Naghel to take over command of the regiment. Just as he assumed control, a bullet struck and killed him.

With Strong still in the field hospital, the 83rd was scrambling for someone to lead them. Captain Hugh Campbell took over, but he was nervous about what to do, especially with the flood of Confederate soldiers racing toward them.

General Butterfield came back to the front and was able to encourage the Third Brigade by grabbing their battle flag and waving it. Still, the only thing Butterfield could do to save his brigade was to lead his soldiers in retreat. A few soldiers from the 83rd took personal items from McLane's body to send home to his family, but they were forced to leave the body. Confederate soldiers buried him later that evening.

The battle was brutal. One-third of the 83rd's force was killed, wounded, or captured. The survivors limped back to a spot called Savage's Station, where it was safe enough to camp for the night. As at Hanover Courthouse, General Butterfield had distinguished himself in battle, and would later be awarded the Congressional Medal of Honor for his bravery at Gaines' Mill.

After the Civil War was over in 1865, members of the 83rd went back to Gaines' Mill to find Colonel McLane's body. After they dug it up, McLane's remains were placed in a coffin and sent back to Erie to be buried in the Erie Cemetery. Mostly through the efforts of McLane's wife, Rosanna, he was promoted posthumously to brigadier general. Today, a school district serving the Pennsylvania boroughs of McKean and Edinboro bears the name "General McLane." It is also the name of the school district's high school.

From his sickbed, Strong could hear the sounds of battle, but he was too weak to get out of bed. He worried about his regiment and prayed that the number of casualties would be low. When a wounded soldier from his regiment was taken to the field hospital, Strong seized his chance to get details.

"Private Watkins, how's the Eighty-Third doing?" he asked.

"It's bad back there, Lieutenant Colonel. We started out by knocking the Rebs back into the woods time and again, but then a whole bunch of 'em attacked us at once. We mighta done better, but the First Brigade ran in retreat, and we were left to take 'em on all by ourselves."

"What about Colonel McLane? Is he still leading the boys?"

"Colonel McLane got shot and killed, and we had to leave his body on the battlefield. Major Naghel got it, too. I remember a time when we couldn't find any Rebs to fight. We even made a joke about it with you, but we sure saw a lot of 'em today."

"I've got to get out there tomorrow," Strong said. "The regiment needs me."

"Lieutenant Colonel, you look awful. I don't think you'll make it into your saddle, let alone lead the boys still out there."

"I'll be all right. I just need a good night's sleep."

In the morning, Strong tried to get dressed. The doctor came in and yelled at him.

"You're too sick to go anywhere. Now get back in bed before you kill yourself!"

"Doctor, I don't care how I feel. I'm needed by my regiment."

The doctor won the argument and forced Strong back to bed. But after he left, Strong called for his assistant and told him to bring his horse to the tent. When he saw his horse outside, Strong made a valiant effort to get up, finish getting dressed, and climb in the saddle. He took off for Savage's Station and his soldiers.

"Hey, here comes the Lieutenant Colonel Vincent," one soldier said as Strong reached the 83rd. The rest of the regiment cheered. "How are you feeling, sir?"

Right as Strong was about to respond, he passed out and fell off his horse.

"Quick!" Captain Campbell yelled. "Get a stretcher over here and take Lieutenant Colonel Vincent back to the field hospital."

Strong remained unconscious as they returned him to the hospital tent, where doctors discussed his condition.

"That darn fool tried to go back to his troops," one said.

"What do you think that we should do with him?" another asked.

"When he wakes up, he's liable to try and head back to his regiment again. I say we put him on the next boat back to Washington. If he makes it, some home cooking might help him recover, and if he doesn't get better, at least they can bury him in their family plot."

"There's a boat leaving at one o'clock. I'll make sure Vincent's on it."

Strong remained unconscious as the boat headed back down the York River. Whether he would live or die was still in question.

CHICKAHOMINY FEVER
—— 1862 ——

As Strong floated toward Washington, he alternated between consciousness and unconsciousness. Once when he came around, a nurse was helping him. Young and pretty, she had brown hair, a nice smile, and a soothing voice. She was putting cold compresses on his forehead to help bring down his fever.

"There you are, sleepyhead," the nurse said. "We're trying to bring down your temperature. The last time that I checked it was over 103 degrees."

"Where am I? Can I go back to my regiment?" Strong asked.

"You're on a boat headed for Washington. I'm afraid your regiment is quite a few miles back. We're going to try and get you home. Where is home, soldier?"

"My name is Lieutenant Colonel Strong Vincent. Call me Strong. I'm from Erie, Pennsylvania."

"Got a lot of family back there?"

"My wife, Lizzie, lives with my parents and my brother and sisters. We got married just as I enlisted. I really miss her."

"Aw, that's nice, Strong. Here, try to sip a little water. You're losing so much liquid through sweat. I don't want you to become dehydrated."

"Thank you. Am I gonna be all right? I saw several soldiers in my regiment die from this fever."

"The ship doctors are taking good care of you. Then you'll get excellent help at a hospital in Washington or in New York City. Now you lie still, and I'll stop back in to check on you later." The nurse squeezed his hand and then was off helping another sick soldier.

Worried about inflammation, the doctors on the boat decided to use a procedure called "leeching," wherein a live leech was placed on Strong's body to suck out blood and get the blood flowing more regularly and remove any inflammation.

As Strong's temperature stayed high, the same nurse returned again and again. Every time that he awakened, she seemed to be there.

"I can't thank you enough for such excellent care," Strong told her.

"That's my job. I'll tell you what—I'll make sure to send a telegram to your family when we get to port. You'll switch boats at Washington and board one headed for New York City. I'll tell your wife to meet you there."

He tried to thank the nurse, only to slip back into unconsciousness.

Back in Erie, the Vincents were sitting down to dinner when suddenly, there was a knock at the door. It was Jimmy, the twelve-year-old boy who worked at the telegraph office delivering messages.

"Mrs. Vincent, I got a telegram for you," he told Lizzie. "It's from Strong."

As she read the telegram, Lizzie's hands started shaking. With tears in her eyes, she looked at BB.

"It's about Strong," she said. "He has some kind of disease. They're taking him to New York City by boat. They want me to meet him there."

"I'm sure he's gonna be all right," BB said, trying to console Lizzie. "They wouldn't put him on a boat if he was deadly sick. Get packed, and we'll head to New York together."

Before leaving, Lizzie sent a telegram to her sister, Sarah, to meet them at the New York City harbor. They arrived at Harbor Landing in New York at almost exactly the same time as Strong's boat. He was immediately taken to the nearest hospital.

"Look at him, Dad," Lizzie said to BB. "He's so thin and pale. Do you think that he's gonna make it?"

"He's in the hands of good doctors now, Lizzie. They'll make him better."

Sarah arrived at the hospital with her husband, Theron Doremus. Lizzie introduced them to BB. Sarah was alarmed at Strong's condition. She also was concerned at the flood of patients being admitted in the hospital.

"Lizzie, it looks like the New York hospitals are overcrowded with patients from the war," Sarah told Lizzie and BB. "Why don't we ask if we can take Strong across the river to a hospital in Jersey City? You and your father-in-law can stay with us, and it would be easier to visit Strong."

"We'd love to have you, Lizzie," Theron said. "This way, you don't have to spend money on a hotel and food. You two can stay with us for as long as you like."

The army approved Strong's move to Jersey City.

As soon as he was admitted to the hospital across the river, Strong's fever broke, and everyone was more optimistic of his recovery. But they still had a long road ahead of them.

Even though BB stayed with the Doremuses, Lizzie would not leave her husband, insisting on sleeping in a chair next to Strong's bed.

"Come back to my house," Sarah begged her sister. "You're looking so weak. I'll stay here and be with Strong. You should get at least one good night's sleep in a comfortable bed."

"I can't leave him," Lizzie said. "If he wakes up, I want him to see me and know things will be all right. He looks so helpless, like a little child."

The doctor arrived, interrupting the two sisters' conversation. "The next two weeks are crucial," he said. "If Strong can make it through them, he has a good chance of survival. We'll do everything we can to get him through this period."

"Please don't let him die, Doctor," Lizzie pleaded.

Strong continued to fight for his life. He showed signs of recovery one minute, only to take a turn for the worse the next. Still, his wife never left his side, nor did the family stop praying.

Strong made it past the couple of weeks the doctor said were pivotal, and he showed signs of getting better.

"Lizzie, I wasn't sure that I would ever see you again," he said.

"You were so sick, Strong. The doctors took good care of you, but it's been a hard couple of weeks. I'm so happy to see you awake and talking."

"You look tired. Have you been here with me the entire time?"

"I couldn't leave your side. I wanted to be here when you awoke. Your dad is at Sarah's house. He'll be by soon to check up on you. Oh, Strong, I didn't know if I was going to lose you. I was so worried."

"I'm going to be all right, Lizzie, especially now that I see that you are here."

Three weeks after Strong arrived at the hospital in Jersey City, the doctor told BB and Elizabeth that he could go back home. Strong was still weak, but perhaps being back home would help in his recovery.

"Thanks for being there for me, Sarah," Lizzie said. "I don't know what I would've done without your help. I'll keep writing to let you know about Strong's condition."

"You're welcome, Lizzie," Sarah replied. "I just wish he was a little stronger before they let you take him home."

Strong, Lizzie, and BB boarded a train that went from New Jersey to Albany, New York. When they reached Albany, the three were set to transfer to a train to Buffalo, but BB saw that Strong seemed especially weak from the travel.

"I don't know if we should take the train to Buffalo right away, son. Why don't we take a day for you to recover?"

"Dad, I want to get home. I know I'll recover faster with Mom's cooking."

"I think that maybe Strong is right, Dad," Lizzie added. "We'll watch him more carefully on the trip and make sure he is taken care of."

Strong and Lizzie ended up winning the argument, but when he got to Buffalo, he again took a turn for the worse.

"This time I am not taking no for an answer," BB said. "We'll check in to the hospital and let you rest before making the last segment of the trip home."

"Dad, I appreciate your concern for me, but we're so close to Erie. Please, let's get me home. I know you mean well, but I just want to be home. I promise I'll be all right."

Again, Strong won out, but BB sent a telegram to his wife to let her know of Strong's condition and when to expect them. By the time the three arrived in Erie, a crowd had filled the depot to greet Strong. Strong's mother and his sister, Rose, ran up to the stretcher carrying Strong. He was still too weak to walk on his own, but Strong's face lit up at seeing members of his family again.

"Mom, I didn't know if I'd make back to see you again," he said.

"Strong, you look so weak. Please don't talk—just rest. You don't know how happy you made me just by making it back home."

He was not out of the woods yet. Strong took another turn for the worse as the disease affected his kidneys and urinary tract. The simplest touch caused great pain, even though Dr. Charles Brandes worked diligently to cure the inflammations. Dr. Brandes had been the family physician for many years, and he worked his hardest to save Strong's life.

By the end of July, Strong Vincent had endured Chickahominy Fever for over one month. He spent August attempting to recover enough strength to return to the war.

When Strong Vincent and the 83rd had won victory at Hanover Courthouse, the Union army had been twelve miles from Richmond. But then, with every battle McClellan fought, his army was losing ground. After the Seven Days battles, during which General Lee held the initiative, the Union Army was back at Harrison's Landing on the James River again. This was where the Union army had started the Peninsula Campaign almost four months earlier.

At that point, President Abraham Lincoln reassigned virtually all of McClellan's troops to Major General John Pope. When General Pope led the Union Army against General Lee and the Confederate Army at the old Bull Run battlefield in late August, the result was even worse than the original battle, as again, the Confederates sent the Union soldiers on the run. Lincoln reinstated General McClellan as the leader of the Union Army.

Strong was healthy enough now to follow the war through stories in the Erie newspaper. The Second Battle of Bull Run had been particularly tough on the 83rd Pennsylvania. More than ninety soldiers were killed, wounded, or captured in the fighting. When he read the story, Strong wanted to race back to Virginia, but Dr. Brandes, Lizzie, and BB talked him out of it, insisting he needed more time to recover his strength before returning to the fight.

"One good thing that happened after the last battle is that General McClellan has returned to lead the army," Strong told his father.

"Do the soldiers like him?" BB asked.

"General McClellan is the one who made us into an army. I think every member of the Eighty-Third would follow him anywhere."

But it was McClellan who was being forced to follow General Lee and the Confederate Army. When Lee brought his troops into Maryland, the two great armies met along Antietam Creek. It turned out to be the bloodiest day in American history, with over twenty-two thousand soldiers killed, wounded, or missing.

Strong was stunned when he read reports of the battle and learned that the 83rd did not fight at Antietam; they were a part of a reserve unit McClellan refused to use.

After that, Strong was determined to return to his men, as it had been almost three months since he came down with Chickahominy

Fever, but Dr. Brandes convinced him to stay one last week in Erie.

Finally, the big day arrived for Strong to return to his regiment. Another big crowd gathered at the depot as he prepared to leave.

"Lizzie, thank you for helping me get back on my feet," he said. "I'll miss you an awful lot after spending so much time together."

"Well, get out there and win this war so we can spend the rest of our lives together," she joked. The two embraced one last time.

Strong boarded the train to Maryland, where the 83rd was camped. He had historic adventures ahead of him.

THE BATTLE OF FREDERICKSBURG

—— 1862 ——

On October 1, Strong Vincent finally rejoined his regiment. The soldiers of the 83rd were happy to see him, especially because he brought twenty-five new recruits with him.

As Vincent looked around, he sadly noticed that many of the soldiers he had helped train at Hall's Hill near Washington were no longer with the regiment, having been killed or severely wounded. But the soldiers here now were hardened, battle-tested veterans.

After Colonel McLane's death and Strong's departure, the 83rd leadership had passed to Captain Orpheus Woodward, but the soldiers voted to reinstate Strong when he returned. Shortly after, he earned a promotion to colonel, whereupon he selected Private Oliver Norton as his aide. Norton told Vincent that the 83rd hadn't moved very far from the Antietam Battlefield. The battle had taken place on September 17.

General Butterfield was no longer leading the Third Brigade, having left it to take charge of the Fifth Corps. Colonel Thomas Stockton, who had previously led the 16th Michigan regiment, took his place. The Third Brigade had also gained a new regiment, the 20th Maine, led by Colonel Adelbert Ames.

The members of the 20th Maine were a tough bunch. Not only did they enjoy fighting each other, but they also had a habit of sneaking out and stealing from the Southern residents, earning them the nickname of "Butterfield's Thieves," since General Butterfield was still in charge when the 20th was added. Having so little action after Antietam was playing into the Maine soldiers' bad habits.

Second-in-command of the 20th Maine was Lieutenant Colonel Joshua Chamberlain. Before enlisting, Chamberlain was a professor of rhetoric and modern languages at Bowdoin College in Brunswick, Maine. Since Chamberlain was assigned to study the same battle tactics books that Strong had studied in Washington, Strong decided to pay a visit to the ex-professor.

"Lieutenant Colonel Chamberlain," Strong said in introduction, "I'm Colonel Strong Vincent of the Eighty-Third Pennsylvania."

"Glad to meet you, Colonel," Chamberlain answered.

"I see Colonel Ames has you reading tactics books. I had to do the same thing for General Butterfield, who was strict in my learning. I had tests almost every night."

"Yeah, Colonel Ames is watching me closely, too."

"Well, let me know if you are having problems with anything. I know what you're going through. Good day, Lieutenant Colonel."

"Good to meet you, Colonel."

On November 10, President Lincoln fired General George McClellan for his inactivity. On the day after McClellan was relieved of his duties for the second time, members of the Fifth Corps, including Strong and the 83rd Pennsylvania, went to his tent to tell him goodbye. As he left the camp, the soldiers cheered, many yelling out that they believed he would lead them again sometime in the future.

Taking over as head of the Army of the Potomac was General Ambrose Burnside, who Lincoln hoped would fight one more battle before making winter camp. Armed with a plan he felt would destroy Confederate General Robert E. Lee's army, Burnside moved his army south toward Fredericksburg, Virginia.

Three miles north of Fredericksburg, the 83rd made camp and received so many new supplies that some soldiers assumed this was to be their winter camp.

"Colonel, should we start having the soldiers make their quarters to prepare for winter?" Private Norton asked Strong.

"No, I think General Burnside's plan is to cross the Rappahannock River and attack the Confederate Army as soon as possible. Winter quarters will have to come later."

The problem was getting across the river. Although Burnside instructed engineers to build a pontoon bridge for the army to cross, this turned out to be harder than expected, as the engineers received constant fire from the Rebels. By December 11, the bridge was finally constructed, and the soldiers, including the 83rd Pennsylvania, marched over to the outskirts of Fredericksburg, where they set up camp on a hill.

Strong went out to examine the area that would become the battlefield. Private Norton came with him. In front of the town of Fredericksburg sat an open field, and in the middle of that field was a sunken road created for laying railroad track. On the other side of the sunken area was an open stretch that ultimately rose fifty feet to the top of Marye's Heights. On top of the hill was a low brick wall, behind which was another sunken road. Taken all together, this made the Confederates' defensive position very strong, especially with their fifty cannons.

"It's an almost invincible position," Strong told Norton. "We're gonna lose a lot of soldiers trying to take those heights, and I don't know if we can do it."

"Do you think General Burnside will pull back?" Norton asked.

"He spent too much time getting us across that river. We'll be attacking in the morning."

"Even if we lose a lot of soldiers?"

"Yeah, once you've got the plan made, you've got to follow it through. Even if it doesn't look so good for your soldiers."

The 83rd camped on the hill for the night. It got so cold that there was a layer of frost on their blankets when the soldiers woke up on the morning of December 13. The mood was somber as the soldiers made coffee and ate a breakfast of hardtack.

Then Strong ordered the regiment to fall in line, and the men of the 83rd readied themselves for whatever lay ahead.

The first assault on Marye's Heights came around noon. From the 83rd's position, Strong and his men could see the whole battlefield. As the Confederate Army unloaded a vicious barrage of artillery and rifle fire, the first attack did not make it up the hill. A second and then third attack suffered similar results. The open area before the hill was littered with dead and wounded soldiers. The men of the Third Brigade gasped as the next group made their attack.

"How many groups do you think Burnside'll throw up there before he realizes the hill can't be taken?" one of the soldiers asked.

"Each wave gets a little bit closer to the wall," Strong answered. "He'll keep sending up more soldiers until someone finally reaches it."

"What if nobody does?"

"Then he'll send up another group and hope that it's the one that makes it."

With the clouds thickening, the sunlight began to wane as wave numbers five and six tried to make it up the hill.

"Colonel, do you think we'll get called on to attack today?" Private Norton asked. "You know at Antietam, we stood around all day ready to go in, but never did."

"I think we're going any time now," Strong said.

A little after three o'clock, the Third Brigade was told to move into position by marching down to the outskirts of the town of Fredericksburg. Colonel Stockton came over to give Strong the orders for his attack.

"You see that white building toward the top of the hill?" he said.

"Yes, sir," Strong answered.

"That's your goal. The Third Brigade will be on the far left of the next attack. The Forty-Fourth New York will be on the extreme left, the Eighty-Third in the middle, and the Sixteenth Michigan will be on your right. Behind you will be the Twelfth New York, the Twentieth Maine, and the Seventeenth New York. Do you understand? I want you to take charge and lead the Third Brigade."

"Yes sir. I'll guide 'em right up to that white house. You can count on me."

"Good luck, Colonel, and God bless."

As the Third Brigade moved through Fredericksburg, they witnessed the damage done the night before, when Union soldiers had looted the town. Furniture and clothing littered the streets. It looked like a tornado had ripped through town.

The Confederate artillery had been firing at the land on the edge of Fredericksburg all day. When they saw the Third Brigade line up, they shelled the area even more intensely.

"Get down!" Strong yelled to his soldiers. Every one of the men followed the order immediately. Fragments from the cannonballs flew at the huddled masses, wounding some men before they had even begun to attack.

During a short lull in artillery fire, Vincent yelled, "Get up, boys!" He took out his sword and turned to the soldiers. "It's time to move forward, Third Brigade!"

The soldiers from all six regiments sprang to their feet and marched forward amid a new wave of cannon fire. Soon, the soldiers reached the sunken area where the railroad tracks were. While they had stayed in formation to this point, many soldiers began to split off as they climbed up the other side of the trench. Strong stopped and got everyone back in proper order.

"Forward to that white house on top of the hill!" he yelled, and the soldiers roared their agreement.

When they hit the open area, the Third Brigade had to make their way through the dead and wounded from previous assaults. Some of the wounded soldiers grabbed at the pants legs of Vincent's soldiers and cried out, "Don't go! You'll only get shot like me." The younger soldiers were aghast.

Strong raced over to the hesitant soldiers. "You've got to keep moving forward!" Strong yelled.

"I'm scared, Colonel," one of them cried out.

"We all are, but you can't stand here, or you'll get shot. Now keep moving forward."

That day, the soldiers of the 83rd learned that making Strong Vincent their leader was the right decision. He stood defiant in the face of the enemy, pointing his sword toward the Rebel army and encouraging his soldiers to keep going. Bullets flew all around him, but Strong didn't seem to care. His leadership encouraged the soldiers to keep going.

Onward the Third Brigade moved. As they were now in rifle range, bullets kept flying, and soldiers fell left and right.

"Keep going, boys!" Strong shouted as a bullet whizzed by his head. "We can make it! Close up the ranks!" Soldiers around him took courage that their leader stood defiant in the midst of enemy fire.

With nightfall coming on, it was harder to see the enemy, but still the soldiers advanced. They were only twenty yards from reaching the white house, but each step was costing a greater number of lives.

Not wanting to take any more casualties, Strong yelled to the soldiers. "Everyone, get down! Try to take cover." Soldiers fell to the ground. "Use your bayonets to dig a hole to protect yourself."

The soldiers still needed something to hide behind, and there was only one thing available on the battlefield—the dead bodies of fallen Union soldiers.

"Try to get as low as you can," Vincent ordered. "You might want to get closer together. Remember how cold it was last night?"

There they were—lying on the battlefield, protected by dead bodies, no food or water, and the temperature approaching the freezing mark. As it got dark, the rifle fire began to slow, and a new noise filled the side of the hill: the sound of the wounded soldiers crying out in pain. It was loud and sad, but the soldiers couldn't do anything for the wounded without risking being shot themselves.

When it got dark, General Lee brought out his sharpshooters, giving the marksmen orders to shoot at any sign of movement.

To add to the evening's horror, when the Rebel sharpshooters opened fire, their bullets often hit the dead bodies protecting the soldiers. The noise it made was sickening. Years after the Civil War was over, many soldiers that survived that ordeal reported that they would still wake up in the middle of the night hearing that ghastly sound."

"Colonel, what's gonna happen to us?" Private Norton asked.

"We have to make it through the night," Strong said. "General Burnside will send another group in the morning to help us get down the hill. Don't worry. Everything will be all right."

"But it's so cold. We'll all freeze to death on this hill."

"Keep calm, Private Norton. You can make it to the morning."

But making it to the morning was no easy task. Between the moaning of soldiers and the noise of bullets striking the dead bodies, morning seemed so far away. There was no sleeping that night. The soldiers huddled together to stay warm.

Strong and Private Norton huddled together. Although he was trying to portray an air of calmness and assuredness, Strong was worried about how he was going to be able to lead the soldiers safely down the hill. He prayed for the courage to lead his soldiers confidently. He also prayed that he would be able to see Lizzie again.

After midnight, a soldier from the 20th Maine jumped to his feet, grabbed his rifle, and then screamed at the Confederate soldiers. He fired a shot and ran right toward the enemy army. Four or five sharpshooters cut him down after only a few steps. Those who saw the spectacle were shocked.

"Did you see that, Colonel?" Private Norton exclaimed.

"Yeah, that was a terrible scene for the troops to witness. My guess is that he probably couldn't take the noises and the cold anymore. It's sort of like a suicide," Strong answered.

"We're all gonna die here, ain't we?" Norton bemoaned.

"Private Norton, you gotta believe that General Burnside will rescue us. It's when you give up hope, like that soldier did, that you let death in. We're gonna be all right," Strong said calmly.

In the morning, however, there was no new group of soldiers. General Burnside had offered to lead the eighth attack himself, but the other officers talked him out of it.

Stuck on the hill, the soldiers were forced to stay in position. To their surprise, apart from a few fired artillery shells in the morning, there was little action, leading some to wonder if the Confederate soldiers were observing the Sabbath, since it was a Sunday.

Some of the soldiers on the hill decided to have some fun. They would hold up a hat on a stick to make Lee's sharpshooters fire. When they blew the hat off of the stick, the soldiers laughed.

One of the soldiers of the 83rd sneaked over to Strong. "Colonel, can we take a bunch of empty canteens back down the hill and get water?" he asked.

"Aren't you worried about being shot?" Strong answered.

"We found a ravine to our left, sir. We could sneak over to it, and that would provide us cover. We can sneak down the ravine back to where we can find water. Can we try, sir? Everyone is really thirsty."

"We could all use a little bit of water to help get us through the day, but the mission looks dangerous. You can try, but be careful. Good luck."

The soldiers' plan worked; they were able to sneak down the hill, get water, and sneak back up without being fired upon. Then they passed around the canteens so that everyone could get at least a sip.

In the afternoon, a group of Confederate soldiers attempted to get around the Union's left flank. If they succeeded, they would be able to fire from the back while the soldiers behind the wall fired from the front—a dire situation.

"Colonel, do you see what they're doin'?" Private Norton asked.

"Yeah, I see 'em," Colonel Vincent said. "Men, we have to move our position so we're facing our left. Don't forget about the Rebel sharpshooters as you maneuver."

The soldiers turned and aimed their rifles at the enemy flanking party.

"Let 'em have it!" Strong yelled.

The soldiers of the 83rd opened fire, and the enemy quickly turned around and headed back for the safety of the brick wall.

"It feels good to make them run in retreat for once," Strong told Norton.

In the darkness of night, a message from Colonel Stockton was passed up the line, ordering Strong to lead the Third Brigade off the hill. The soldiers began rustling around, getting their things together.

"What are you all doing?" Strong called out.

"Didn't you get the message, Colonel? We're supposed to retreat."

"Not now. I'll tell you when," Strong responded as the soldiers grumbled.

"Colonel Vincent, sir," Norton said. "The soldiers are complaining. Do you hear 'em?"

"Yeah, I hear 'em. We'll wait a bit. Trust me."

There was a full moon that night. It lit up the side of the hill. If Strong started the retreat at that point, he would lose a lot of soldiers. Off in the distance, however, he saw a line of clouds, and they were moving toward his soldiers. He decided to wait until the clouds were finally overhead and blocked out the light of the moon, plunging the hill into darkness.

Strong turned to his soldiers. "Now we can go. Move quietly so that you don't get the Rebs firing at us."

When the Third Brigade finally left the hill, no one was injured. Happy to get off Marye's Heights, the soldiers cheered for Colonel Vincent.

"I'm always gonna listen to that Colonel Vincent's orders," said a soldier in the 44th New York. "He wants to keep us alive!"

The 83rd lost thirty-seven soldiers during the battle, some to wounds and some to death. If Strong hadn't called off the attack and told his soldiers to take cover, that number would have been much higher. Strong showed that he was a great leader, not only to the soldiers of the 83rd, but to all of the other soldiers of the Third Brigade.

LAWYER IN WASHINGTON
— 1863 —

Not long after the fiasco at Fredericksburg, President Lincoln fired General Burnside and promoted General Joseph Hooker to be the commander of the Army of the Potomac. When Hooker took over, his first action was to raise the morale of the army: he improved the medical services and made sure the soldiers got better food. Another thing he did was to provide furloughs which enabled Strong to be able to return to Erie and see his wife and family.

When Strong got home, he told his father of his experience in the study, away from Lizzie and Strong's mother. He didn't want either of them to hear how close he'd come to death.

"Spending the night on that hill was the scariest time in my life," Strong told his father. "The only thing I kept thinking about while I was on that hill was Lizzie. Thoughts of her and a whole lot of prayers were what got me through that experience. One positive thing that came out of the Battle of Fredericksburg is that I feel the soldiers have more confidence in my leadership."

"That must've been a harrowing experience," BB said. "It was smart to tell me of the battle in here, away from the women. So now you have a new leader. What do you think of General Hooker?"

"His nickname is 'Fighting Joe.' He has really helped build back morale. There's just one thing that bothers me about him."

"What's that, son?"

"There are rumors that a group of generals meet at his headquarters every night and drink to excess. Another rumor says ladies of the evening pay visits every night, too. You never brought us up to be like that."

"Do you think he will be a good leader in spite of his behavior?"

"I guess there's nothing that says a general has to maintain proper morals to be a great leader. We really need a victory over General Lee, though."

Strong spent a few weeks back at home. He valued every minute he could spend with Lizzie.

"You were pretty secretive about what happened in that last battle," Lizzie said one day when they were riding horses in the country. "I'm a big girl, Strong. I want to know everything that's happening to you."

"I know, but I didn't feel comfortable telling you how scary the situation was. I want our visits to be enjoyable. We have such little time together."

"I love riding out here in the fields with you, Strong. I wish that we had more time to be together. I worry so much about you when you are gone."

"I'll be all right. Every night before I go to sleep, I think of you and when I will see you again. I hope we win this war soon so that we can start our life together."

"What will you do when you have to go back?"

"We're in winter camp, so we try to stay as warm as we can." Strong took a deep breath.

The two halted their horses and sat down in the tall grass.

"Sometimes I forget about how beautiful the fields of Pennsylvania are. I could stay sitting here with you forever," Strong said as he took Lizzie in his arms.

"We'll have plenty of time to be together once this war is over. Promise me you'll always tell me what happened to you in future battles. I want to know everything going on with you in your life."

"I'll try, Lizzie, but sometimes the experience is so brutal. We probably should be getting back home. I really enjoy our time alone together, and I hate for it to end."

After a few days, little Jimmy from the telegraph office came to the door again.

"I have a telegram for you from Washington, Mr. Vincent. Is it from Mr. Lincoln?" Jimmy asked.

"No, Jimmy. It's from some lawyer. Thanks for bringing me the message."

"What is it, son?" BB asked.

Strong read the message. "Judge Joseph Holt wants me to go to Washington during the winter break and be a lawyer for a few cases involving crimes committed by soldiers." Holt was from Kentucky, and he had worked hard to keep his state from joining the Confederacy. For all of his efforts, Abraham Lincoln appointed him as judge advocate general, and later he was put in charge of the Bureau of Military Justice.

"Are you still going to be a soldier?"

"Yeah, Dad. This is only while the soldiers are in camp. I guess there are too many cases to deal with, and they need another lawyer to help. When I am finished in Washington I'll probably go back to my regiment."

Strong decided to follow the orders of Judge Holt and prepared to resume his legal career for the few months of winter camp time. The following day he went to the train depot. Lizzie came to see him off.

"I have a little present for you, Strong." Lizzie handed him her rider's crop. "This is to remind you of our special times riding together. Now that you're on a horse all day, you're going to need it. When you use my rider's crop, think of me and how much I love you."

"I think of how much I love you all of the time," Strong said, then he hugged her close. "Thank you for the gift. I'll cherish it."

As he boarded the train, Strong did not know it at the time, but he would never see his wife again.

When Strong got to Washington, he learned he would be working on several different cases, defending some soldiers charged with disorderly conduct, some charged with disobeying their superior officers, and some charged with theft. Guilty verdicts for these crimes often meant intervals of hard labor or fines.

One of the most common types of case was desertion. Soldiers who left their unit were made to appear before a trio of judges. If found guilty, they would be kicked out of the army, but first their sentences would be written up and read in front of crowds of people. Stripes, buttons, and military insignias would then be ripped off their uniforms.

Strong worked hard for the soldiers he represented. The case that brought the most notoriety was one where Colonel Hiram Berdan accused Lieutenant Colonel Caspar Trepp of cowardice on the battlefield. If he was found guilty, Trepp would be kicked out of the army. Trepp came to Strong's office to discuss his defense.

Caspar Trepp was born in Switzerland, where he grew up, trained to be an expert marksman, and served in an elite sharpshooters' outfit in the French Foreign Legion. He fought in the Crimean War. In the late 1850s, Trepp immigrated to the United States and settled in New York City. When the Civil War broke out, he enlisted in the Union Army. Noticing there were no sharpshooting regiments in the army, he put forth the idea to start one. Hiram Berdan was a famous marksman before the war, and he used his influence to form the 1st US Sharpshooters Regiment.

Nevertheless, there was friction between Trepp and Berdan, because Berdan wanted everyone to believe that he had thought up the idea of a sharpshooter regiment. The accusation of cowardice came as a result of their tension.

"Good morning, Lieutenant Colonel. Please have a seat," Strong told his client. Trepp saluted Vincent, and then sat down. "Tell me a little about why you are accused of cowardice."

"Colonel Vincent, I am originally from Switzerland, but came to the United States about five years ago. When your Civil War began, I enlisted and suggested that a sharpshooter regiment be formed. I admit that Colonel Berdan had the name and reputation needed to form the

First US Sharpshooters, but he wants to take credit for the full idea. He is saying that I showed cowardice on the battlefield because he knows if I'm found guilty, that I will be discharged from the army. Then there will be no one to dispute his claims."

"Are his accusations warranted?"

"No. You can ask any of the soldiers in the regiment. They'll tell you I have never shown cowardice. They'll also tell you that Colonel Berdan doesn't know what's happening on the battlefield because he never goes out on the battlefield. He's a great marksman, but he is a terrible soldier and a worse leader."

"Okay, Lieutenant Colonel. Let me speak with the other soldiers in your regiment. I'll see what they have to say."

As Strong interviewed the soldiers who would be his witnesses, each one said that Lieutenant Colonel Trepp was a great marksman and a courageous leader, but each one also said they would not testify to that in a trial. They were too afraid of repercussions from Colonel Berdan. They also said that they would not back Berdan's accusations that Trepp showed cowardice, either.

At the trial, Strong brought in witnesses who spoke of Colonel Berdan's petty jealousies. He also pointed out how no soldier had provided testimony proving Berdan's allegations of Trepp's cowardice. The three officers acting as the matter's judges ruled that with only Berdan's complaints given as evidence, Lieutenant Colonel Trepp was not guilty of cowardice on the battlefield.

Not long after the trial, Trepp was given leadership of a separate unit entirely made up of Swiss-born sharpshooters. Although still under Berdan's leadership, Trepp never had any more problems. At Gettysburg, the 1st US Sharpshooters played a key role in helping the Union to maintain control of Cemetery Ridge. Trepp was later killed at the Battle of Mine Run in November 1863.

A few weeks after the Trepp trial, Strong was summoned to Judge Holt's office.

"Please have a seat, Colonel Vincent," Holt said.

"Thank you, sir," Strong responded.

"I'll tell you why you are here. I've been watching you in court, and I feel that you are an excellent lawyer."

"Thank you. I had very good training back in Erie."

"I have a proposition for you," Holt said. "I would like to keep you here in Washington, where you will be promoted to judge advocate general. You'll try cases and also sit with other advocate generals to judge cases. You can even bring your wife here to Washington to stay with you. I see that you were married right after you enlisted, and you probably haven't spent a lot of time together. Staying in Washington will give you the opportunity to make up for that. So, what do you say?"

"That is quite an offer," Strong answered. "I am certainly honored by it. But I feel I must say no. I enlisted in the army to fight. I have a regiment of soldiers down in Virginia who are awaiting my return so that I can lead them in future battles. Thank you again for such a distinguished offer."

"But, Colonel Vincent, think of your wife. She probably worries about you every day. If you accept my offer, she wouldn't have to worry about you being a casualty on the battlefield anymore."

Strong thought of Lizzie. He remembered how much she loved being in Washington in the spring of 1862. It was a hard to say no to the prospect of being with Lizzie all of the time, but Strong had already made up his mind long ago to see this war through.

"Yes, I would love to spend time with my wife, but she knows why I have chosen to fight rather than to stay in Erie and continue my law practice. I am sorry, sir. I love this country, and I want to fight to see that it is made whole again."

"All right, Colonel. There are a few more days of the court session, and after that you'll be dismissed to join your outfit in Virginia. If, however, you change your mind during these last few days, my offer will still stand."

"Thank you, but I don't think I will alter my plans to be reunited with the Eighty-Third Pennsylvania."

THE BATTLES OF CHANCELLORSVILLE AND MIDDLEBURG

— 1863 —

When Colonel Vincent arrived at the winter quarters in April, the soldiers of the 83rd greeted him warmly. It had been a cold winter, but General Hooker had done his best to provide his troops with the food and clothing necessary to allow the soldiers to make it through as comfortably as possible.

General Butterfield, who had been in charge of the Fifth Corps, was named Hooker's chief of staff. Replacing Butterfield was General George Meade. The Third Brigade was still led by Colonel Stockton.

On April 27, General Hooker moved his troops, believing that he had a plan that would destroy Lee's army and take his own army right to Richmond.

The Union Army marched down to the Rappahannock River and then crossed it on a pontoon bridge as they headed for the crossroads of Chancellorsville, Virginia.

The Third Brigade was short one of its regiments. With numerous cases of smallpox, the 20th Maine did not march to Chancellorsville. That left the 83rd Pennsylvania, the 44th New York, the 16th Michigan, the 12th New York, and the 17th New York.

The Fifth Corps was assigned to the extreme left of the Union line. On May 1, the soldiers marched into their position. The next morning, Strong had the regiment chop down trees and dig out an area for their defense. General Meade rode by, checking the work of his soldiers. When he got to the 83rd's position, he stopped to talk to Strong.

"This looks really good, Colonel," he said. "Do you think you can stop the enemy's attacks?"

"The Rebs better not try to attack us, General, or they'll meet with a lot of casualties. We're not going to give up this position."

The soldiers gathered by their defensive works right as cannons began to fire—the signal for the start of the battle.

All day long, the soldiers caught glimpses of battle, but their position was never attacked. Strong sent a few soldiers out as a skirmish line to find the location of the Confederate Army, but all they met were enemy skirmishers looking for Union soldiers.

Two days later, on May 3, the Fifth Corps moved to a new location closer to the action. When they got to the new position, Strong ordered the soldiers to use picks and shovels to dig out a new defensive line.

Still, they did not see the enemy. The soldiers learned that things were not going very well for the Union Army. Lee had divided his army in two, attacked, and driven Hooker's army back.

The next two days saw the Fifth Corps move again, but by that time both the Union and Confederate Armies were tired enough that Hooker moved his troops out of Chancellorsville and back across the Rappahannock River. It was another defeat for the Army of the Potomac. Morale, which was so high before the battle, had sunk back to post-Fredericksburg levels.

The soldiers made camp and passed the days in drill and sentry duty. The 12th New York's and 17th New York's enlistments had expired, so they were taken out of service, leaving the Third Brigade with just four regiments. General Griffin left as head of the First Division, and General James Barnes replaced him. Colonel Stockton also left, and Strong took command of the Third Brigade. He had shown himself to be an excellent leader, and now he would take charge of the four regiments of the brigade. Captain Orpheus Woodward was promoted to take over Strong's old job as head of the 83rd Pennsylvania.

After his victory at Chancellorsville, General Lee planned to move his army north to attack Pennsylvania, but he kept a few soldiers back to make General Hooker think he was still in Virginia. Lee used the Blue Ridge Mountains to hide his troops, counting on the cavalry led by General J. E. B. ("Jeb") Stuart to keep the Union cavalry from pinpointing the exact location of the Southern army. By June, however, General Hooker had learned of Lee's northward movement.

On June 13, Hooker began to move his army north. It took the Union soldiers three days to reach Manassas Junction, carrying their heavy backpacks though the hot sun and humid air that held no trace of a breeze.

On the fifth day of Union troop movements, June 20, the sun was especially hot, and clouds of dirt choked the soldiers as they made their way north. At night, the regiment finally pulled into a place called Gum Spring. When they got there, soldiers dropped everything and raced to the water.

The Union cavalry commander, General Alfred Pleasonton, was assigned to find out General Lee's location. As both armies headed north, Pleasonton and Confederate General Jeb Stuart faced off in a series of battles. After one in Aldie, Virginia, the Rebel cavalry retreated westward to Middleburg. To defeat the Confederates there, Pleasonton decided he needed infantry, and made a request to General Meade.

Meade called Strong to his quarters.

"Colonel Vincent, I want you to take your Third Brigade and head to Middleburg and support General Pleasonton," Meade said. "When you get to Middleburg, you will follow orders given by the general."

"Yes, sir," Strong responded. "Will we leave right away?"

"Have your troops ready to march by three o'clock in the morning."

Strong went to find the leaders of his four remaining regiments, only to learn that Colonel Joshua Chamberlain, who was now in charge of the 20th Maine, was sick with sunstroke. After assigning Lieutenant Colonel Freeman Conner of the 44th New York to lead the 20th Maine at Middleburg, Strong went to call on Chamberlain to see if he was all right.

"Lawrence, I hear that you're not feeling well," Strong said, calling him by his middle name, which Chamberlain preferred.

"Yeah, I can't believe that all of my soldiers made that last march without incident, but their leader was the one who went down. I hear the brigade is going into battle."

"We're going to help General Pleasonton in a battle against the Confederate cavalry. I assigned someone from the Forty-Fourth New York to take over your regiment. Your soldiers will be in good hands."

"Is there something bothering you, Strong? You look a little distressed."

"This is the first time that I will lead the brigade into battle. I've seen what happens when a leader makes a mistake—a lot of lives are lost. I don't want to lose soldiers needlessly."

"Strong, there is one thing about you that I am particularly impressed by. I've watched you look over a piece of ground and almost instantly know how best to use it in battle. What's really impressive is that you never went to West Point to learn warfare. It seems to come naturally to you. I don't think you have to worry about needless casualties."

"Thanks, Lawrence. That helps me feel more confident in my leadership. I'll check in on you when we return."

At three o'clock the next morning, Strong had the troops up and moving, starting their march over the eleven miles to Middleburg. The 83rd complained the entire way, having lost sleep after a hard day of marching. Strong heard the whining but kept the regiment moving forward. By seven o'clock, the Third Brigade reached Middleburg.

Strong rode forward to talk to General David Gregg, one of General Pleasonton's commanders.

"There they are," Gregg said, pointing out the position of the Confederates. "They're dug in behind a short wall at the top of the hill. That's not Jeb Stuart, it's General Fitzhugh Lee. He's one of Bobby Lee's relatives. I want you to attack the forces and get them up and fighting. If I try to move my cavalry against them all dug in like that, they'll tear us to pieces. I'll be watching, and when it's time for the cavalry to attack, I'll lead them in. Do you understand what I want you to do?"

"Yes, sir. I'll get those Rebs up and moving," Strong answered.

When Gregg left to take care of his soldiers, Strong looked out over the field. There was a wide-open area of some two or three hundred yards that his soldiers would have to cross to get to the hill where the Confederates had dug in behind the stone wall and created strong defensive position, aided by their one cannon. To Strong, it looked like a miniature version of Fredericksburg, and he did not want to experience those kinds of losses again.

To his right, Strong saw a wooded area that ran all the way past the left end of the Confederate line. Just as Colonel Chamberlain had observed, when he saw that line of trees, Strong knew exactly what to do. He called for the leaders of the four regiments.

"All right, here's what we're going to do. I want the Forty-Fourth, the Sixteenth, and the Twentieth to assemble here. Be careful, because that cannon is starting to find the correct range. Me and Captain Woodward will take the Eighty-Third into the woods over there." He turned to Colonel James Rice, who was leading the 44th New York. "I want you to be in charge of the three regiments. You have to wait a little bit before starting across that field in front of us. It'll take us a little while to maneuver through the woods. The Eighty-Third will attack their left flank, and you'll attack the front. If you leave too early and we aren't close to the jumping-off point, the Rebs will cut you down."

The three regiments began lining up to cross the open field as the 83rd slipped into the woods.

"We have to move quickly, but we can't make a lot of noise. I don't want the enemy to know we are here until we attack," Strong said to his troops.

They moved quietly, but when they were still a little way from the Confederate line, the sound of rifle fire was heard.

"Quickly, men. Colonel Rice has started to lead the troops across the field. I'll run ahead to find a good place to attack from."

As soon as Strong found the left end of the line of Confederate soldiers, he spotted General Fitzhugh Lee. He was standing with another officer, and the two of them were laughing.

Go ahead and keep laughing, Strong thought. In a few minutes you won't think it's so funny. As his soldiers reached the point of attack, Strong called to them.

"When you come out of the woods, I want you to make lots of noise! Let them know their left flank is about to be crushed!"

The 83rd went barreling out of the woods, yelling and firing their rifles, and the Confederates were taken completely by surprise.

As the entire left end of the Confederate line collapsed, there was no smile on General Lee's face, only a look of horror. Lee tried to move soldiers around to fight the 83rd, and at that moment Strong's three other regiments crashed into Lee's front line. Bullets flew in all directions.

True to his word, General Gregg led the cavalry at the enemy when he saw that Strong's men had gotten the Confederates up and out of their dug-in position. With soldiers attacking his troops from all sides, all General Lee could do was order his soldiers to retreat. The Confederate cavalry ran to their horses. Their infantry soldiers started running.

As the enemy retreated, Strong got all of his regiments back in order. The Confederates had left their cannon, so Strong ordered the 16th Michigan to fire it at the retreating Rebels. Then the Third Brigade began a long chase.

Two or three times, Lee stopped his soldiers and tried to dig in, but the Union Army quickly overran them. After a few miles, they were able to cross a creek and dig in behind a rock wall on the other side. Gregg called a halt to his cavalry.

"Work your magic again, Colonel Vincent," he told Strong.

Again, after a brief survey of the land, Strong instantly knew what to do.

"The Sixteenth will attack with the Eighty-Third over the creek's bridge," he ordered. "The Forty-Fourth and the Twentieth will cross the creek and attack on the banks."

When Vincent gave the order to attack, the 16th Michigan and the 83rd Pennsylvania yelled out that they were going to grab as many prisoners as they could and then charged over the bridge.

The soldiers who went across the creek struggled to get up the muddy far bank. But when they did, they met up with the regiments that had crossed the bridge, and chaos ensued. Again, the only thing General Lee could do was order his men to run.

General Gregg came over to Strong. "Excellent work, Colonel Vincent."

"General, my soldiers are exhausted. We can't go on any further."

"Colonel, take your injured soldiers and your prisoners back to the town. We'll push Lee a little further, and then we'll meet back up with you. You led your soldiers very well."

Colonel Strong Vincent's leadership not only kept the number of casualties low (two killed, eighteen wounded); it resulted in taking over two hundred prisoners.

The soldiers of the Third Brigade remained in the area for a couple of days before making their way back to rejoin the Fifth Corps. On the march, Strong heard a couple of soldiers of the 20th Maine discussing his leadership.

"That Colonel Vincent sure knows how to lead soldiers," one said.

"That had to be the most exciting battle we'll probably ever get into," another answered, and then they stopped when they saw Strong riding past.

"Three cheers for Colonel Vincent!" they yelled, and the rest of the 20th Maine showed their respect by joining in the cheer.

As Vincent came up to the 83rd Pennsylvania, he remembered how the soldiers had complained when they were awakened to march to Middleburg. Now their mood had changed. They were laughing and having a good time.

"Hey, Colonel Vincent!" one soldier called out as Strong rode by. "Find us another battle like that last one."

A second soldier laughed. "Yeah, that was the most fun that I've had since I joined this here regiment."

When they reached the place where the Fifth Corps was located, the soldiers of the Third Brigade made their camp. Strong was resting in his tent when his aide, Private Norton, interrupted him.

"Colonel, General Meade is out here and wishes to speak to you."

Strong hurried outside and saluted General Meade.

"Good evening, General."

"Colonel Vincent, I've been talking to General Gregg, and he gave you all of the credit for the success at Middleburg. I want to commend you on a fine job."

"Thank you, General, but we couldn't have succeeded without the cavalry's help."

"Colonel Vincent, if you keep fighting like you did, I promise I will make sure you are promoted to general. This army needs more fighting men like yourself."

"Thank you, sir," Strong said, starting back to his tent.

"Just think, Colonel Vincent. We'll have to start calling you General Vincent!" Private Norton said before he ducked in.

Strong smiled.

A few weeks after their meeting, General Meade replaced General Hooker as the head of the Army of the Potomac. After the fighting on the second day of the Battle of Gettysburg, General Meade would hear of the next courageous action undertaken by Strong Vincent. Keeping his word, he would send a telegram to Abraham Lincoln asking him to promote Colonel Vincent to General Vincent. But the promotion would come under circumstances neither Meade nor Strong would celebrate.

THE BATTLE OF GETTYSBURG

—— JULY 2, 1863 ——

After the Battle of Middleburg, the Army of the Potomac resumed its march north at a faster pace. The Confederate Army had crossed the border into Maryland and was racing toward Pennsylvania.

The soldiers woke up early each day, quickly made coffee, and had a breakfast of salt pork and hardtack. Then, after making sure they had full canteens of water, they began the day's march. The weather was hot and humid, and when the area they were marching through contained a spring or creek, soldiers eagerly ran to it and refilled their canteens. At the end of the day, the soldiers made a quick dinner and looked for a place to sleep. The soldiers mostly slept on the ground with no shelter, except if it was raining. Each day the soldiers marched twenty tough miles, only resting on June 26 and 27.

Lincoln replaced General Hooker with General George Meade as head of the Army of the Potomac on June 28. General George Sykes was promoted to replace Meade as the Fifth Corps' leader. Starting on the same day, Sykes had the corps up and marching each morning.

The longest march the Fifth Corps made came on July 1. The soldiers started in northern Maryland. At some point, the soldiers would be marching into Pennsylvania, and Strong was looking forward to being back in the Keystone State. As they approached the border, he went over to his flagman, Sergeant Alexander Rogers.

"Sergeant, when we cross into Pennsylvania, unfurl your flag. I'll have our band play 'Yankee Doodle.'"

As they crossed the border, the soldiers of the 83rd Pennsylvania were excited. "We're back home!" came the exuberant shouts as local residents came out to cheer on their heroes and offer them baked goods. Strong pulled his horse to the side of the road to watch as the other regiments crossed into Pennsylvania, catching the same sense of excitement. It was the happiest he and his soldiers had seemed in a long time; their attitudes had been so dreary from all of the marching.

As they were watching the spectacle, Strong turned to Lieutenant John Clark and said, "What death more glorious can any man desire than to die on the soil of old Pennsylvania fighting for that flag."[1]

"Colonel, with a big battle coming up, do you really wanna talk about death?" Clark responded, and Strong grinned.

Strong kept his soldiers moving forward, as they needed to arrive in the town of Hanover by nightfall, still some fourteen miles away. When they arrived, the townspeople celebrated, partly because a Confederate cavalry unit had recently ridden through, causing panic. Now Union soldiers had come to town.

Women were dressed in red, white, and blue. They sang "The Star-Spangled Banner" and brought the soldiers water and milk to drink and fruit to eat, overwhelming the men with their demonstrations of kindness.

The soldiers made camp just outside of town. They had marched twenty-six miles that day.

It wasn't long before General Sykes called the division and brigade leaders together. Strong went to the meeting as his men were settling down to sleep.

"I got some news. Today, the First and the Eleventh Corps fought General Lee's forces in a town called Gettysburg, and General John Reynolds was killed. General Meade wants us to march into Gettysburg tonight and be ready to fight Lee first thing in the morning. I know we just had a hard march today, but we're going to have to wake up the men and be on the road as soon as possible."

Strong told his soldiers to get ready as fast as they could. Each brigade of the Fifth Corps tried to line up first and have the honor to lead the soldiers to battle. Even though they had marched so many miles that day, the men got ready for more without complaint. They could hear the canons firing from Gettysburg.

As the corps came to each small town before reaching Gettysburg, citizens came out and greeted them by singing the Star-Spangled Banner. The cheers and refreshments from the people helped the soldiers keep moving, but they were all in need of a little sleep.

"The men look really haggard," Private Norton said to Vincent.

"I know, but we have to keep them moving. If they stop, they'll probably drop to the ground and fall asleep."

"How can they be expected to fight after all of the marching and very little sleep?"

"Don't worry Private Norton. When we are about to face the enemy and the soldiers know they're fighting for Pennsylvania, how tired they are will be the last thing on their minds."

When they were less than five miles from Gettysburg, General Sykes decided to give the soldiers a break. It was between one and two in the morning. All of the soldiers instantly dropped to the ground and fell asleep. After a few hours of rest, Strong told Private Norton to play reveille on his bugle to awaken them. The soldiers struggled to their feet, and somehow, they finished the march. It was between seven and eight o'clock in the morning when they reached Gettysburg.

As they arrived, General Sykes met with the Fifth Corps division and regiment leaders.

"General Meade is keeping us in reserve. He doesn't know when or where Lee will attack, so we'll stay right here and wait for orders to move."

To Strong, this was good news. He called the Third Brigade's four regimental leaders together.

"Tell the soldiers they can make breakfast. They may even be able to get a quick nap. The most important thing I want done is for each regiment to send out a few details to fill canteens from the creek we just passed. It's going to be another hot one, and the soldiers will need water."

Little did Strong know that water would play a big part in the upcoming battle.

While the Fifth Corps was resting, General Meade positioned the rest of the army atop a line known as Cemetery Ridge, one corps after another. The effect was a solid wall of defense. Toward the left end of the line was the Second Corps, led by Major General Winfield Scott Hancock.

That left room for one more group of soldiers to line up on the ridge; that was the Third Corps, led by Major General Dan Sickles. But as Sickles led his soldiers to the left flank, he spotted high ground right in front of where he was told to place his corps. Without approval from General Meade, Sickles moved his corps to occupy this high ground, which created two problems. The first was that Sickles' soldiers were all alone a half-mile ahead of the rest of the army back on the ridge. The second was that the end of the line, a place called Little Round Top, was left completely unguarded. If the Confederates got around Sickles' men, they could run to the top of the hill and outflank the entire Union Army.

General Gouverneur Warren was Meade's engineer, tasked with making sure every corps was in the correct position. When he got to Little Round Top, he saw that General Sickles was moving his forces out ahead of his designated position. He raced back to find General Meade, but it was too late to relocate Sickles' soldiers because the Confederate attack was beginning. Meade had to find soldiers to support General Sickles' line, and he had to get them there in a hurry.

General Sykes's Fifth Corps was no longer in reserve. They were ordered to help Sickles' men. That still left Little Round Top unguarded. General Warren went to General Sykes for help.

"General Sykes, I need a brigade or two of soldiers to move as quickly as possible to cover that hill over there," Warren said excitedly as he pointed to Little Round Top.

"We're still waiting to find out where Meade is going to place my troops, but I'll get General Barnes to send a brigade right away," Sykes answered.

General Sykes told his assistant to ride around and find General Barnes as fast as he could. The assistant rode around, but he could not find General Barnes.

Strong was waiting with the Third Brigade along with the rest of the Fifth Corps. He and Private Norton saw Sykes's assistant riding around swiftly and rode out to meet him.

"What seems to be the problem?" Strong asked. "You're racing around here frantically."

"I need to find General Barnes! Do you know where he is?"

"I have not seen him. What are your orders?"

"General Sykes wants General Barnes to send soldiers to that hill over there," the assistant said.

Strong instantly understood the urgency to place soldiers on that hill. "You don't have to look for General Barnes. I will take my brigade there."

"Colonel, you can't do that," the assistant said. Army protocol dictated that while a general can place a colonel's troops on the battlefield, a colonel cannot move his soldiers without the general's knowledge. By breaking this rule, Strong could be arrested, face a court-martial, and possibly end up in a military prison for many years.

But Strong understood the severity of the situation. "I will take full responsibility for taking my brigade there," he said, and then went to find Colonel Rice of the 44th New York.

"Colonel, I want you to be in charge of taking the Third Brigade over to that hill. Private Norton and I will ride ahead to find the best place to put each regiment. You need to hurry. I don't think we have that much time before the Rebs attack."

"I'll get the soldiers there as fast as I can, Colonel Vincent," Rice said.

Strong and Norton raced over to Little Round Top, which rose above the surrounding valley. Next to it was Big Round Top, a hill 130 feet taller, but it was overgrown with trees while Little Round Top had been cleared of forestation. That made the smaller hill the key to the Union defense.

Little Round Top had one thing that would help Strong's brigade—boulders. The sides and top of the hill were littered with large rocks, leftovers from a previous ice age. They helped to make the defensive position stronger, as soldiers could shoot from behind them for protection, and the enemy would have to try to cross over them as they charged. When adding that to the steepness of the hill, Strong believed he could hold off the Confederate attackers.

When Strong looked down from the top of the hill, he instantly noticed one thing that General Sickles had not taken into account: Little Round Top was the most important piece of ground on the entire battlefield. No general would ever court-martial him for taking the initiative in bringing his brigade there without proper notice.

As he was looking over the ground, a cannon shell flew close to where Strong and Norton were. That was followed by a second shot.

Strong examined the area and saw that the Confederates were firing cannons from a ridge at him from a little ways away. He looked over and saw that Private Norton had the brigade's flag flying in the breeze.

"Private Norton, get that flag down. You wanna get us killed? Get down from your horse and stand behind one of those big rocks!" Strong yelled angrily, then got off his horse to figure out where he should position his troops.

Strong had two choices of how he could place his soldiers. He could clump all of them together on the top of the hill to fight off any advancing enemy troops, or he could use the terrain to position each regiment one after another in a semicircle around Little Round Top. As Colonel Chamberlain had previously observed, after Strong looked at the landscape, he instantly knew the best way to use a piece of ground in battle. He would use the terrain in front of him to align his brigade. They could use the rocks for protection as they fired at the enemy.

Hearing the brigade coming, Strong went over to where his defensive line would start.

The first regiment to arrive on the scene was the 44th New York. The 16th Michigan was right behind them. Strong went over to the hill's far right end, where he would position the 44th.

"Colonel Rice, I want your regiment to anchor next to this big rock, then start spreading out to your left. The Sixteenth Michigan will line up next to you."

"Colonel Vincent, may I have a word?" Colonel Rice asked. "In all of the battles we have fought together, the Forty-Fourth has always been next to your Eighty-Third. Remember back on the Peninsula when we were 'Butterfield's Twins'? I request permission to have my boys fight next to yours."

"All right, Colonel Rice. Pull your regiment back and let the Sixteenth Michigan cut in front of you. Then swing around the Sixteenth to begin your line. But do it quickly!"

"Thank you, Colonel Vincent. My soldiers take courage from the way the Eighty-Third fights."

The 16th Michigan was now the right flank of the brigade's line. Next to them was the 44th New York, and then came the 83rd Pennsylvania. That left the 20th Maine on the far left of the line. Strong got on his horse and rode over with Colonel Chamberlain to look over the Maine men's position.

"Well, Lawrence, this is where I am placing your line. You are the extreme left end of the entire Union defense. You'll probably receive attacks from your front, and they may move to your left if the enemy tries to outflank you. All of the regiments have the same orders not to retreat, but it is vital that your troops do not retreat. You're going to have to fight until the last man. Good luck to you and your men."

"And to you too, Colonel Vincent," Chamberlain said.

Strong had placed all of his regiments. As he dismounted his horse to take one last look to see how his troops were situated, Private Norton approached.

"You know, Norton, I'll either earn that promotion to general today or this will be my last battle," he said.

"Don't be talking about death just before a battle, Colonel," Norton answered. "Seeing that this is sure to be a tough battle, I request permission to take the flag back by the rocks and grab a rifle to join the boys on the line."

"I think we'll need you. Go over and tell our musicians to grab rifles, too."

Less than fifteen minutes after Colonel Strong placed Chamberlain's men, the Confederate soldiers of General John B. Hood attacked. Had the young brigade commander waited for General Sykes's assistant to find General Barnes, as he was supposed to do if following army regulations, no one would have been defending Little Round Top when the Confederates moved to take it. The Union Army would have been outflanked, and its chance of winning the Battle of Gettysburg would have been in extreme jeopardy.

The 16th Michigan was the first regiment to notice the Rebel soldiers coming up the hill. Lieutenant Colonel Norval Welch, their leader, yelled for his soldiers to fire into the enemy. The first blasts of the battle for Little Round Top sent the Confederates running back down the hill, leaving a number of dead and wounded soldiers behind them.

Hood's men now knew two things: one, there were Union soldiers posted on top of that hill, and two, the Confederates outnumbered the Union soldiers by a huge amount. The amount was almost two to one.

Strong looked around and realized something disturbing—he had been so busy placing the regiments that he had forgotten to take care of his horse. Not wanting the horse to get shot by a stray bullet, he yelled to Lieutenant Daniel Clark to have someone take the horse to the rear. Then he told Clark to go and see if he could find General Barnes and have him send more troops to Little Round Top.

As Strong gave orders to Lieutenant Clark, an enemy bullet crashed into a nearby rock. Clark called out to him.

"Colonel Vincent, you can't stand that far forward! Those soldiers on the rocks down there are trying to hit you." Sharpshooters in the Confederate line were aiming at officers.

"I'll be fine," Strong answered. "I have to stand forward to keep my eye on the battle."

Captain Woodward had positioned the 83rd so that one line would fire into the enemy, move back, and then a second line would come up and fire. After the first attack, the Confederates moved more to the center, where the 44th and the 83rd were stationed. As the enemy came back up the hill, they cried out their characteristic Rebel yell.

Captain Woodward waited as they got closer and closer. Then he shouted, "Fire!" and the first line blasted away. He repeated the order for the second line. When the smoke from the gunfire cleared, the Confederates were heading back down the hill. The fire from the 83rd had been particularly deadly.

The Confederates re-formed their lines and came back up the hill.

"Fire at will!" Woodward yelled to his soldiers, and the battle was on.

When they attacked for the third time, the Rebel soldiers made it farther up the hill. Both sides fired away, but the positions Strong had given his soldiers helped both the 83rd and 44th deliver heavy blows without taking many casualties. The two Union regiments were not going to leave their spot as long as the Confederates kept attacking.

When the enemy made their next onslaught, some of the Rebel soldiers found boulders to hide behind and fire from. As it became difficult to drive them out from their cover, casualties on both sides increased.

Strong moved across the defensive line, putting reserves wherever a hole had formed due to wounded or dead soldiers. A bullet hit the rock to his left, another gift from the sharpshooters. The Rebs knew that if the Union soldiers lost their leader, they might panic. Someone yelled back to Strong that he should move farther back, where it was safer, but Strong would not take cover; he continued to lead his brigade.

The battle continued, bullets flying in both directions. The Confederates continued to try to charge up the hill, only to be beaten back by Strong's men. Still, Strong was losing soldiers to enemy fire, and he knew that to win the battle he was going to need reinforcements. His smaller brigade could only hold off the larger enemy force for so long.

Another bullet buzzed by Strong's head into the rocks behind him. The aim of the sharpshooters was getting better.

Then a new problem appeared. Strong's troops were running out of ammunition. Word went down the line to make every shot count. There wasn't anything to spare.

Strong sent a courier, Private Jim Reynolds, over to see how Colonel Chamberlain was doing. Reynolds reported back that the 20th Maine's defensive position had less protection than the other three regiments. The hill they were fighting behind wasn't as steep, and there weren't many boulders to use for cover. They were also fighting a group of Alabama soldiers, part of Brigadier General Evander Law's brigade, who had never been driven from the battlefield before.

"Colonel Vincent, the Twentieth Maine is putting up a fierce resistance. They're forcing the Alabamians back down the hill on each charge. But they're also running out of ammunition and are resorting to getting bullets from their dead and wounded soldiers."

"Thank you, Private. I knew the Maine regiment would put up a good fight. The problem is that without reinforcements, we can lose this hill."

The Confederate soldiers began to move a little to their left, where they crashed into the 16th Michigan forces. Holding the right end of Strong's defense, the 16th Michigan's position was also more vulnerable due to its sparser terrain.

As the Confederates made another charge at the right end of the brigade's line, some of the Michigan boys turned and ran to the rear. If he lost the 16th Michigan, the whole battle could be over; the Confederates would go running right through the gaping hole in his defense. Strong had to keep the 16th together and fighting. He made a mad dash to try to stop the soldiers from running.

The retreating Michigan soldiers had run into a member of the 44th New York who was injured and being taken to the rear to a field hospital.

"Didn't you hear what Colonel Vincent said?" the injured soldier yelled. "There's no retreat. Get back on the line."

Strong quickly ran over to the injured soldier and said to the members of the ambulance corps, "Take this man to the field hospital. I'll take care of this," Then he turned to the Michigan soldiers. "My order was no retreating. What are you all doing?"

"Colonel, there are so many of 'em, and we're running out of ammunition. We can't hold 'em back," one of the soldiers said.

Strong was holding the rider's crop Lizzie had given him. He always carried it to help position the soldiers. Taking the crop, he whacked the 16th Michigan soldier standing closest to him and growled, "Get back on that line, and if I see you run again, I'll grab a rifle and shoot you myself!"

Suddenly more afraid of their colonel than the enemy, the Michigan soldiers turned around and ran back to their line.

Strong was in trouble; he knew that. He had to find a way to keep his soldiers in their defensive position until reinforcements arrived, which meant he had to think of something that would encourage them to stay and fight. He quickly thought of a way. He would take his sword, jump up on one of the rocks, and yell something to inspire his troops.

Strong reached down to get his sword, but it wasn't there. He reached all around his waist, and still he could not locate it. Where was it? Then he remembered he had left his sword on his horse. He was so busy positioning his troops that he had forgotten to remove it from where it was connected to the saddle. The horse was taken to the rear, and so there was no sword to use in his plan.

Strong looked down at the rider's crop in his right hand. He would have to use the rider's crop instead of the sword. He suddenly remembered his wife's last words to him: When you use my rider's crop, think of me and how much I love you. Strong knew what he was about to do was risky. The chance that he might get shot was good.

He thought again of his wife. "I love you, Lizzie," he said. "I always will."

Then off he ran to encourage his troops.

When Strong got back to the defensive line, the Confederates had gotten even farther up the hill. Locating a jutting rock toward the middle of his line, Strong climbed up.

He took the rider's crop, pointed it at the enemy, and shouted angrily to his soldiers, "Don't give an inch!"

The soldiers, especially the 83rd and the 44th, all yelled out, gave the most ferocious look, and fired into the enemy. It was a deadly barrage of bullets to honor their leader. Down went a great number of Confederates.

But being on the rock, Strong was exposed to the enemy, especially to the sharpshooters that had been firing at him all day. One of their shots finally hit him, sending him off of the rock.

A soldier ran over.

"Take me over to the woods," Strong told him. "Do not take me back to the field hospital. We can't afford to lose a man." As a couple of soldiers placed him on a stretcher, Strong said, "This is the fourth or fifth they have shot at me, and they have hit me at last."[2]

Strong was taken over to a tree in the woods near the end of the 83rd's and the beginning of the 20th Maine's line. But the situation was getting worse. When Vincent went down, the 16th began panicking once again.

Just as the situation was getting hopeless, reinforcements finally arrived. After talking to General Sykes, General Warren had found Colonel Patrick Henry O'Rorke, the leader of the 140th New York regiment. O'Rorke, like Colonel Vincent, never went to his commanding general to report that he was taking his soldiers somewhere; he raced the regiment to Little Round Top as fast as he could.

As soon as the 140th arrived on the hill, O'Rorke saw where his soldiers were needed the most. He yelled for them to reinforce the area by the 16th Michigan. But as he was pointing the way his soldiers should go, a bullet fired by the enemy struck him in the throat, and Colonel O'Rorke was killed instantly. Still his troops strengthened the line's right flank.

The next time the Union soldiers blew the Confederates back down the hill, and they did not come back. That part of Strong's line had held, but Colonel Chamberlain's 20th Maine's left flank was still in danger.

While the 83rd was still fighting on the right side, Chamberlain asked Captain Woodward if he had any soldiers he could spare. Captain Woodward told him no, but he would stretch his line out farther to help the 20th Maine.

On their next charge, the troops from Alabama broke through Chamberlain's defense. The two groups fought at close range and even in hand-to-hand combat. By some miracle, the Maine men pushed the Confederates back down the hill. The problem was that their ammunition, even that taken from the dead and wounded, was almost gone.

Chamberlain had a real dilemma. He didn't have enough ammunition to stay and fight where he was, but his brigade commander, Colonel Strong Vincent, had told him that he must not retreat. He couldn't stay where he was, and he couldn't retreat. There was really only one place to go: forward.

His troops were in a formation that looked like an "L." The long part of the letter fought off attacks to his front, while the base fought off attacks to his left flank. What Chamberlain wanted to do was swing the soldiers in the base around like a swinging door and then have them run down the hill. The problem was that when he yelled, "Bayonets!" his soldiers got excited and ran down the hill without any other order. Some of the soldiers in the 83rd ran down with them, but Captain Woodward quickly cut them off and told them to go back to the top of the hill. If Chamberlain's charge did not work, they would be needed to fight the soldiers the Maine men had been fighting all day.

Fortunately, Colonel Chamberlain had luck on his side. The soldiers from Alabama were like the Third Brigade in that they had to march many miles that day to get to Gettysburg. But unlike Strong's brigade, they had not made sure they all had full canteens of water. The soldiers were not only exhausted, but they were very thirsty. When first told to attack, their leader, Colonel William Oates, refused to make his soldiers charge until they had water. Oates sent a detail to fill some canteens, but on their way back, members of the 2nd US Sharpshooters Regiment captured them.

When the Rebel detail failed to return from filling their canteens, Colonel Oates was forced to order the Alabama soldiers to go ahead and attack. Many soldiers went down; bullets from the 20th Maine's guns shot down some, but others fell from extreme dehydration.

After the last attack where they had broken through the Union line, Colonel Oates was thinking of retreating. All of a sudden, he saw Chamberlain's men running down the hill like madmen. Some of the Alabama soldiers tried to stay and fight, some took one shot and retreated, but most ran. As they retreated, they ran right into the 2nd US Sharpshooters Regiment. They opened fire on the Confederates and then took a great many prisoners of war.

Colonel Chamberlain's gamble paid off. He somehow miraculously saved the left flank of Little Round Top. The left end of the Union defense was secure.

However, it was Strong's bold move to take the Third Brigade to the hill without authorization that helped to save the second day of the Battle of Gettysburg for the Union Army. Showing up only fifteen minutes before Hood's troops attacked, he led his soldiers fearlessly. But leading from the front caused his injury. Now Strong was fighting a different battle—one to save his life.

A NOBLE DEATH
—— JULY 7, 1863 ——

After the fighting on Little Round Top had been decided, Strong was taken to a field hospital that had been set up at the Bushman farmhouse, two miles away from the battlefield.

The problem was that many soldiers of the 83rd Pennsylvania did not know where he had been taken.

Private Norton had been by Strong's side for a long time, and he went searching for him. When Norton ran into Lieutenant Colonel Welch of the 16th Michigan, Welch gave him a poor excuse for his regiment's behavior during the battle, but Norton was only interested in directions to the field hospital where Strong had been moved. Welch told him how to reach Strong's location.

The Bushman farmhouse was full of dead and wounded bodies, so much so that Norton had to watch where he stepped as he searched for his colonel. The stench was almost unbearable, and the moaning of the wounded reminded him of Fredericksburg.

Strong was in one of the bedrooms on the first floor. Before going into the bedroom, Norton went to talk to the doctor about Strong's condition.

"Doctor, will he make it?"

"I'm afraid not. The bullet entered in the left groin, destroyed everything in its path and ended in the right groin. There are also some broken bones. I can fix the broken bones, but his body is too damaged to make it through surgery. I'm sorry."

The news stunned Private Norton. He didn't want to think about going into battle without Colonel Vincent at his side. He opened the door slowly, and he saw Strong lying on the bed. The room was dark with the curtains closed, and there was only one small bed. Being a tall man, Strong barely fit into it.

To Norton, Strong's room smelled like death.

"Norton," Strong said, holding out his hand for Private Norton to take. "How is the Third Brigade?"

"We're still on that hill, Colonel, and the Rebels have quit attacking, all thanks to you."

Strong smiled. He said little more. He was in pain, but he never showed it. He just held Norton's hand.

The doctor entered the room.

"I have some morphine, Colonel. It should help you with the pain."

Strong showed more life at that point than Norton had seen since he entered. "No morphine!" he yelled out.

"But, Colonel, you have to be in a lot of pain."

"I am, but when I'm conscious, I want to be as alert as I can be," Strong said. "I can handle the pain."

"All right, Colonel. If you change your mind, let me know."

"Colonel, why not take the morphine? It will help," Private Norton said.

"No. I'll be all right."

Norton stayed for a little while before returning to Little Round Top. He would never see his friend and leader again.

Once news got around that Strong's wound was fatal, more members of the Third Brigade came to visit.

"How is he?" asked Private William Connor of the 44th New York.

"Not good. He's been in and out of consciousness all evening," Lieutenant Clark said.

When he saw Strong awaken, the New Yorker said, "Colonel, sir. I'm Private Connor and this here is Private Hamilton. I want you to know that all of us members of the Forty-Fourth feel real bad about your injury. And we are all real mad at who caused you to jump up on that rock and get shot. We have been going over all night to them cowards in the Sixteenth Michigan and giving them what for. We'll make 'em pay; don't you worry."

"Private," Strong said weakly. "I want you to go back to your regiment and tell everyone to stop going over and fighting the Sixteenth. I don't blame them. In war, people get shot. That's what war is. Now promise me that you and your friend will go back to your regiment and stop this foolishness."

The two soldiers sadly left Strong's side and went back to fulfill his order.

On the morning of July 3, General Dan Butterfield, Strong's old commander, came to visit him.

"Colonel Vincent, I was very sorry to hear about your injury. What you did yesterday in running your troops to the top of that hill showed what a great leader you've become. When General Meade heard, he sent a telegram to President Lincoln asking him to promote you to brigadier general. We haven't heard back yet, but General Meade and I know Lincoln will agree."

"Did you hear that, Colonel Vincent?" one of the members of the 83rd said. "We'll have to start calling you General Vincent."

Everyone in the room cheered.

"General," Strong said. "I want to go back home."

Being back home had helped him to recover from Chickahominy Fever. Maybe it would work with this wound, also.

"I'll have two members of your staff prepare you for traveling, and I will alert Captain Woodward of their assignment," Butterfield said.

The soldiers got Vincent ready to move but prodding him in any way was extremely painful for him. Then the doctor came in.

"General, I'm sorry. This man cannot be moved. You saw how the slightest bit of movement causes intense pain. He must stay right here."

"Well, then if I can't go home, can someone send a telegram to let my wife and family know what is happening?" Strong asked. "Maybe my wife, Lizzie, can make it here before I pass."

"Lieutenant Clark, will you send the telegram? Be careful—Confederates are still in the area," General Butterfield said.

"I'll be careful, sir. Don't worry, Colonel Vincent. I'll get the message through."

As Strong hung between life and death, the third day of the Battle of Gettysburg raged and would see what would become known as Pickett's Charge. Around one o'clock in the afternoon, the Confederate Army unleashed a cannon barrage the likes of which the Union soldiers had never seen. When the cannonade ceased, as many as fifteen thousand Confederate soldiers emerged from the woods to attack the center of the Union defense. The attack failed, with Lee's soldiers suffering more than six thousand casualties.

Day three turned out to be the last day of the battle. It was a Union victory, and General Lee had to drag his army back to Virginia.

Due to problems with the telegraph system, it took a few days for Lieutenant Clark's telegram to reach Erie. When it did, Jimmy took the wire over to the Vincent residence. Knowing what the telegram said, Jimmy was crying as he knocked on the door.

"Jimmy, what's the matter?" BB said as he answered the door. Jimmy gave the telegram to him quickly and then ran away, still crying.

BB read the telegram, then stood there, stone-faced.

"BB, what is it?" Sarah Vincent called as she entered the room.

"It's Strong. He's been shot in some place called Gettysburg. The doctor thinks the wound is fatal," BB said, trying hard to keep his emotions together.

Lizzie rushed into the room. She took one look at Sarah's and BB's faces and that told her the news without anyone saying anything. Her knees began to buckle as she sobbed loudly. Sarah grabbed her and tried to comfort her.

"Boyd," BB said, "hitch the horses to the wagon, and then bring it around front."

"Yes, sir," Boyd said, and then he raced to the barn.

"BB, what are you going to do?" Sarah asked.

"I'm going to find this Gettysburg and bring Strong back to Erie."

"I'm going with you," Lizzie said.

"Lizzie, you can't," Sarah said. "You are with child. You go bouncing around in back of that wagon, and you might lose your baby." At the time, Lizzie was six months pregnant.

"Sarah's right," BB said. "Besides, I may be riding into a battlefield. It's no place for a woman."

Lizzie ran into her bedroom, crying loudly.

"She'll be all right. I'll take care of her," Sarah said as she walked to Lizzie's door. Before she went in, however, she turned to her husband. "BB, go and bring our son home."

After gathering some maps, BB took off in the wagon.

Although Strong's final days were painful, he hardly let on. He never cried out in pain, and it was only when he moved that his face showed the agony he suffered. He spent his days between consciousness and unconsciousness, and when he was awake, he was praying.

On the morning of July 7, five days after being shot, it was obvious that Strong's last hours were at hand. He began reciting the Lord's Prayer, but he was never able to finish it.

Mercifully, his life slipped away from him.

Strong's body was carefully embalmed, and then Lieutenant Clark loaded the body in a wagon and started the journey back to Erie.

Later that same day, BB arrived in Gettysburg. After hours spent going from camp to camp, BB finally learned where his son was being held. He still held out hope that he would be able to talk to him before he died. However, when he finally made it to the Bushman farmhouse, Captain Woodward was there to greet him.

"I'm sorry, Mr. Vincent. Your son passed away yesterday. We didn't know you were coming to retrieve his body, so I had Lieutenant Clark take General Vincent back to Erie. General Meade sent a telegram to Washington, and President Lincoln promoted your son to brigadier general before he died. We tried to tell him that, but he was in and out of consciousness so much that I don't know if he ever really understood."

BB was saddened at the news of his son's death. He had ridden so hard to get to Gettysburg to see Strong alive. He thought of Lizzie and how devastated she would be.

Distraught, he said to Captain Woodward, "I guess I'll ride back to Erie alone. I tried to get here as fast as I could, hoping to see him before he died."

"Mr. Vincent, your horses need rest. I'll get 'em some water and some feed. While you're waiting, I'll get some of the boys to take you to the battlefield so you can see where your son gave his life. General Vincent was a great leader, and he did a lot to save the Union Army."

The soldiers eagerly complied with Captain Woodward's order.

"We sure liked Colonel—I mean, General Vincent," one said. "He always worried about saving as many lives as he could in battle. We will surely miss him."

At Little Round Top, BB saw the rock Strong had stood on when he was shot. Tears ran down his cheeks as he tried to picture his son's last actions. The soldiers told him how brave he was to risk his life to encourage them to hold their ground. His sadness was combined with a great sense of pride in son's dedication to his soldiers and country. By the time he got back, his horses were ready to travel again. Both BB and Lieutenant Clark ended up arriving back in Erie the same day.

EPILOGUE

Strong's funeral was held on July 13 at St. Paul's Church. Lieutenant Clark spoke, telling everyone how courageous General Vincent had been. He was then buried in the Vincent family section of the Erie Cemetery.

Elizabeth remained distraught after the funeral, and none of the members of the Vincent family could lessen her grief. One thing that did help her were the letters she received from Miss Porter in Farmington, providing guidance to survive the grieving process. Another thing that helped was that a little less than three months after Strong's death, Lizzie gave birth to a baby girl she named Blanche.

However, Elizabeth was not through experiencing heartache. Just as Blanche was about to turn one year old, she got sick and died. Blanche was buried next to the father that she never knew.

Elizabeth died on April 14, 1914 at the age of seventy-five. She stayed loyal to the memory of her husband and never remarried, even though she was twenty-four years old when he died. Continuing to live with Strong's family, she devoted herself to religious work with Strong's family and, somehow, despite all of the pain she had experienced, became known for the happiness that she brought to others. She always had a smile on her face as she helped those in need. Lizzie was buried next to Blanche and Strong in the Erie Cemetery.

To recognize the importance of their hometown hero, the School District of Erie, Pennsylvania named one of its schools after Strong Vincent.

If you go to the Gettysburg Battlefield today and ask a tourist who Joshua Chamberlain was, chances are he or she can tell you the story of Chamberlain and the Twentieth Maine's charge. Chamberlain not only survived the Battle of Gettysburg, he survived the rest of the Civil War. He attended every reunion at Gettysburg, constantly telling and retelling the story of the Twentieth Maine.

If you ask that same tourist who Strong Vincent was, all he or she might know is that he was the man who placed Chamberlain's troops on Little Round Top. But Vincent was more than that.

One of the soldiers who was with Strong Vincent when he died, Private Amos Judson, wrote about Vincent's leadership and personality. He said:

> And when they [his soldiers] came to witness his skill in handling the regiment, and the brigade, on the field of battle, and how he fought side by side and shared all of the dangers equally with them, the seal of his superiority became stamped upon their hearts.
>
> If he was always first and foremost on the field of battle, it was because his sense of duty took him there, and if he became animated in the excitement of the fray, it was the result of a glorious enthusiasm which rose higher and higher as the joy of battle swelled in his breast and inspired him to do all that might become a man.
>
> To sum up the character of General Strong Vincent in three words, I can only say that he was a gallant soldier, a fine scholar, and a Christian gentleman, and when you say this, you have said all that can be said of any man.[3]

They say that dead men tell no tales. Strong Vincent took his regiment to Little Round Top because he saw how valuable the position was. When some of his men panicked and began to retreat, he willingly gave up his own life to keep his troops in place until reinforcements arrived. When he died, much of his story died with him at Gettysburg—until now.

NOTES

1. Norton, Oliver. *The Attack and Defense of Little Round Top*, Gettysburg, July 2, 1963. 1913 (reprint Gettysburg, 1992) p.285.
2. Judson, Amos. *History of the Eighty-Third Regiment Pennsylvania Volunteers.* p. 67.
3. Judson, Amos. *History of the Eighty-Third Regiment Pennsylvania Volunteers.* p. 72.

BIBLIOGRAPHY

Judson, A.M. *History of the Eighty-Third Regiment Pennsylvania Volunteers*. Erie, Pa: B. F. H. Lynn Publishers, 1865.

Nevins, James H. and William B. Styple. *What Death More Glorious A Biography of General Strong Vincent*. Kearney, NJ: Belle Grove Publishing, 1997.

Norton, Oliver. *The Attack and Defense of Little Round Top*, Gettysburg, July2, 1963. 1913; reprint, Baltimore, MD: Butternut and Blue, 1992.

Schellhammer, Michael. *The 83rd Pennsylvania Volunteers in the Civil War*. Jefferson, NC: McFarland & Company, Inc., 2003.

Vincent, Boyd. *Our Family of Vincents; A History, Genealogy and Biographical Notices*. Cincinnati, Ohio: Stewart Kidd Company, 1924.

www.ingramcontent.com/pod-product-compliance
Lightning Source LLC
LaVergne TN
LVHW041610070526
838199LV00052B/3069